Coast-to-Coast Raves
for *Hocus Pocus*

Continued . . .

Books by Kurt Vonnegut

PLAYER PIANO

THE SIRENS OF TITAN

MOTHER NIGHT

CAT'S CRADLE

GOD BLESS YOU, MR. ROSEWATER

WELCOME TO THE MONKEY HOUSE

SLAUGHTERHOUSE-FIVE

HAPPY BIRTHDAY, WANDA JUNE

BREAKFAST OF CHAMPIONS

WAMPETERS, FOMA & GRANFALLOONS

SLAPSTICK

JAILBIRD

PALM SUNDAY

DEADEYE DICK

GALÁPAGOS

BLUEBEARD

HOCUS POCUS

FATES WORSE THAN DEATH

HOCUS POCUS

KURT VONNEGUT

BERKLEY BOOKS, NEW YORK

This Berkley book contains the complete text of the original hardcover edition. It has been completely reset in a typeface designed for easy reading and was printed from new film.

HOCUS POCUS

A Berkley Book/published by arrangement with the author

PRINTING HISTORY
G. P. Putnam's Sons edition/September 1990
Published simultaneously in Canada
Berkley edition/November 1991

ISBN: 0-425-13021-5

A BERKLEY BOOK® TM 757,375
Berkley Books are published by The Berkley Publishing Group,
200 Madison Avenue, New York, New York 10016.
The name "BERKLEY" and the "B" logo
are trademarks belonging to Berkley Publishing Corporation.

PRINTED IN THE UNITED STATES OF AMERICA

10 9

EDITOR'S NOTE

The author of this book did not have access to writing
paper of uniform size and quality. He wrote in a library
housing some eight hundred thousand volumes of interest to no one else. Most had never been read and probably never would be read, so there was nothing to stop
him from tearing out their blank endpapers for station-
ery. This he did not do. Why he did not do this is not
known. Whatever the reason, he wrote this book in
pencil on everything from brown wrapping paper to the
backs of business cards. The unconventional lines sepa-
rating passages within chapters indicate where one
scrap ended and the next began. The shorter the pas-
sage, the smaller the scrap.

One can speculate that the author, fishing through
trash for anything to write on, may have hoped to estab-
lish a reputation for humility or insanity, since he was
facing trial. It is equally likely, though, that he began
this book impulsively, having no idea it would become
a book, scribbling words on a scrap which happened to
be right at hand. It could be that he found it congenial,
then, to continue on from scrap to scrap, as though each
were a bottle for him to fill. When he filled one up,
possibly, no matter what its size, he could satisfy himself
that he had written everything there was to write about
this or that.

He numbered all the pages so there could be no doubt

about their being sequential, nor about his hope that someone, undaunted by their disreputable appearance, would read them as a book. He in fact says here and there, with increasing confidence as he nears the end, that what he is doing is writing a book.

There are several drawings of a tombstone. The author made only one such drawing. The others are tracings of the original, probably made by superimposing translucent pieces of paper and pressing them against a sunlit library windowpane. He wrote words on the face of each burial marker, and in one case simply a question mark. These did not reproduce well on a printed page. So they have been set in type instead.

The author himself is responsible for the capitalization of certain words whose initial letters a meticulous editor might prefer to see in lowercase. So, too, did Eugene Debs Hartke choose for reasons unexplained to let numbers stand for themselves, except at the heads of sentences, rather than put them into words: for example, "2" instead of "two." He may have felt that numbers lost much of their potency when diluted by an alphabet.

To virtually all of his idiosyncrasies I, after much thought, have applied what another author once told me was the most sacred word in a great editor's vocabulary. That word is "stet."

                                        K.V.

This work of pure fiction is dedicated to the memory of

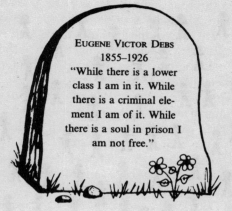

EUGENE VICTOR DEBS
1855–1926
"While there is a lower
class I am in it. While
there is a criminal ele-
ment I am of it. While
there is a soul in prison I
am not free."

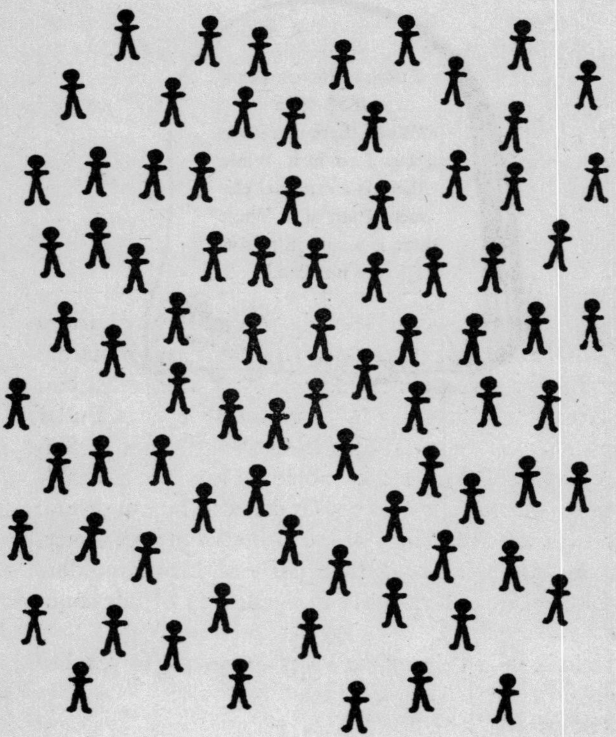

1

My name is Eugene Debs Hartke, and I was born in 1940. I was named at the behest of my maternal grandfather, Benjamin Wills, who was a Socialist and an Atheist, and nothing but a groundskeeper at Butler University, in Indianapolis, Indiana, in honor of Eugene Debs of Terre Haute, Indiana. Debs was a Socialist and a Pacifist and a Labor Organizer who ran several times for the Presidency of the United States of America, and got more votes than has any other candidate nominated by a third party in the history of this country.

Debs died in 1926, when I was a negative 14 years of age.

The year is 2001 now.

If all had gone the way a lot of people thought it would, Jesus Christ would have been among us again, and the American flag would have been planted on Venus and Mars.

No such luck!

At least the World will end, an event anticipated with great joy by many. It will end very soon, but not in the year 2000, which has come and gone. From that I conclude that God Almighty is not heavily into Numerology.

Grandfather Benjamin Wills died in 1948, when I was a plus 8 years of age, but not before he made sure that I knew by heart the most famous words uttered by Debs, which are:
"While there is a lower class I am in it. While there is a criminal element I am of it. While there is a soul in prison I am not free."

I, Debs' namesake, however, became anything but a bleeding heart. From the time I was 21 until I was 35 I was a professional soldier, a Commissioned Officer in the United States Army. During those 14 years I would have killed Jesus Christ Himself or Herself or Itself or Whatever, if ordered to do so by a superior officer. At the abrupt and humiliating and dishonorable end of the Vietnam War, I was a Lieutenant Colonel, with 1,000s and 1,000s of my own inferiors.

During that war, which was about nothing but the ammunition business, there was a microscopic possibility, I suppose, that I called in a white-phosphorus barrage or a napalm air strike on a returning Jesus Christ.

I never wanted to be a professional soldier, although I turned out to be a good one, if there can be such a thing. The idea that I should go to West Point came up as unexpectedly as the finale of the Vietnam War, near the end of my senior year in high school. I was all set to go to the University of Michigan, and take courses in English and History and Political Science, and work on the student daily paper there in preparation for a career as a journalist.

But all of a sudden my father, who was a chemical engineer involved in making plastics with a half-life of 50,000 years, and as full of excrement as a Christmas turkey, said I should go to West Point instead. He had never been in the military himself. During World War II, he was too valuable as a civilian deep-thinker about chemicals to be put in a soldier suit and turned into a suicidal, homicidal imbecile in 13 weeks.

I had already been accepted by the University of Michigan, when this offer to me of an appointment to the United States Military Academy came out of the blue. The offer arrived at a low point in my father's life, when he needed something to boast about which would impress our simple-minded neighbors. They would think an appointment to West Point was a great prize, like being picked for a professional baseball team.

So he said to me, as I used to say to infantry replacements fresh off the boat or plane in Vietnam, "This is a great opportunity."

What I would really like to have been, given a perfect world, is a jazz pianist. I mean jazz. I don't mean rock and roll. I mean the never-the-same-way-twice music the American black people gave the world. I played piano in my own all-white band in my all-white high school in Midland City, Ohio. We called ourselves "The Soul Merchants."

How good were we? We had to play white people's popular music, or nobody would have hired us. But every so often we would cut loose with jazz anyway.

Nobody else seemed to notice the difference, but we sure did. We fell in love with ourselves. We were in ecstasy.

Father should never have made me go to West Point.

Never mind what he did to the environment with his nonbiodegradable plastics. Look what he did to me! What a boob he was! And my mother agreed with every decision he ever made, which makes *her* another blithering nincompoop.

They were both killed 20 years ago in a freak accident in a gift shop on the Canadian side of Niagara Falls, which the Indians in this valley used to call "Thunder Beaver," when the roof fell in.

There are no dirty words in this book, except for "hell" and "God," in case someone is fearing that an innocent child might see 1. The expression I will use here and there for the end of the Vietnam War, for example, will be: "when the excrement hit the air-conditioning."

Perhaps the only precept taught me by Grandfather Wills that I have honored all my adult life is that profanity and obscenity entitle people who don't want unpleasant information to close their ears and eyes to you.

The more alert soldiers who served under me in Vietnam would comment in some amazement that I never used profanity, which made me unlike anybody else they had ever met in the Army. They might ask if this was because I was religious.

I would reply that religion had nothing to do with it. I am in fact pretty much an Atheist like my mother's father, although I kept that to myself. Why argue somebody else out of the expectation of some sort of an Afterlife?

"I don't use profanity," I would say, "because your life and the lives of those around you may depend on your understanding what I tell you. OK? OK?"

I resigned my commission in 1975, after the excrement hit the air-conditioning, not failing, however, to father a son on my way home, unknowingly, during a brief stopover in the Philippines. I thought surely that the subsequent mother, a young female war correspondent for *The Des Moines Register,* was using foolproof birth control.

Wrong again!

Booby traps everywhere.

The biggest booby trap Fate set for me, though, was a pretty and personable young woman named Margaret Patton, who allowed me to woo and marry her soon after my graduation from West Point, and then had 2 children by me without telling me that there was a powerful strain of insanity on her mother's side of her family.

So then her mother, who was living with us, went insane, and then she herself went insane. Our children, moreover, had every reason to suspect that they, too, might go crazy in middle age.

Our children, full-grown now, can never forgive us for reproducing. What a mess.

I realize that my speaking of my first and only wife as something as inhuman as a booby trap risks my seeming to be yet another infernal device. But many other women have had no trouble relating to me as a person, and ardently, too, and my interest in them has gone well beyond the merely mechanical. Almost invariably, I have been as enchanted by their souls, their intellects, and the stories of their lives as by their amorous propensities.

But after I came home from the Vietnam War, and before either Margaret or her mother had shown me and the children and the neighbors great big symptoms of their inherited craziness, that mother-daughter team treated me like some sort of boring but necessary electrical appliance like a vacuum cleaner.

Good things have also happened unexpectedly, "manna from Heaven" you might want to call them, but not in such quantities as to make life a bowl of cherries or anything approaching that. Right after my war, when I had no idea what to do with the rest of my life, I ran into a former commanding officer of mine who had become President of Tarkington College, in Scipio, New York. I was then only 35, and my wife was still sane, and my mother-in-law was only slightly crazy. He offered me a teaching job, which I accepted.

I could accept that job with a clear conscience, despite my lack of academic credentials beyond a mere BS Degree from West Point, since all the students at Tarkington were learning-disabled in some way, or plain stupid or comatose or whatever. No matter what the subject, my old CO assured me, I would have little trouble keeping ahead of them.

The particular subject he wanted me to teach, what's more, was 1 in which I had excelled at the Academy, which was Physics.

The greatest stroke of luck for me, the biggest chunk of manna from Heaven, was that Tarkington had need of somebody to play the Lutz Carillon, the great family of bells at the top of the tower of the college library, where I am writing now.

I asked my old CO if the bells were swung by ropes.

He said they used to be, but that they had been electrified and were played by means of a keyboard now.

"What does the keyboard look like?" I said.

"Like a piano," he said.

I had never played bells. Very few people have that clanging opportunity. But I could play a piano. So I said, "Shake hands with your new carillonneur."

The happiest moments in my life, without question, were when I played the Lutz Carillon at the start and end of every day.

I went to work at Tarkington 25 years ago, and have lived in this beautiful valley ever since. This is home.

I have been a teacher here. I was a Warden for a little while, after Tarkington College officially became Tarkington State Reformatory in June of 1999, 20 months ago.

Now I myself am a prisoner here, but with pretty much the run of the place. I haven't been convicted of anything yet. I am awaiting trial, which I guess will take place in Rochester, for supposedly having masterminded the mass prison break at the New York State Maximum Security Adult Correctional Institution at Athena, across the lake from here.

It turns out that I also have tuberculosis, and my poor, addled wife Margaret and her mother have been put by court order into a lunatic asylum in Batavia,

New York, something I had never had the guts to do.

I am so powerless and despised now that the man I am named after, Eugene Debs, if he were still alive, might at last be somewhat fond of me.

2

In more optimistic times, when it was not widely understood that human beings were killing the planet with the by-products of their own ingenuity and that a new Ice Age had begun in any case, the generic name for the sort of horse-drawn covered wagon that carried freight and settlers across the prairies of what was to become the United States of America, and eventually across the Rocky Mountains to the Pacific Ocean, was "Conestoga"—since the first of these were built in the Conestoga Valley of Pennsylvania.

They kept the pioneers supplied with cigars, among other things, so that cigars nowadays, in the year 2001, are still called "stogies" sometimes, which is short for "Conestoga."

By 1830, the sturdiest and most popular of these wagons were in fact made by the Mohiga Wagon Company right here in Scipio, New York, at the pinched waist of Lake Mohiga, the deepest and coldest and westernmost of the long and narrow Finger Lakes. So sophisticated cigar-smokers might want to stop calling their stinkbombs "stogies" and call them "mogies" or "higgies" instead.

The founder of the Mohiga Wagon Company was Aaron Tarkington, a brilliant inventor and manufacturer who nevertheless could not read or write. He now would be identified as a blameless inheritor of the genetic defect known as dyslexia. He said of himself that he was like the Emperor Charlemagne, "too busy to learn to read and write." He was not too busy, however, to have his wife read to him for 2 hours every evening. He had an excellent memory, for he delivered weekly lectures to the workmen at the factory that were laced with lengthy quotations from Shakespeare and Homer and the Bible, and on and on.

He sired 4 children, a son and 3 daughters, all of whom could read and write. But they still carried the gene of dyslexia, which would disqualify several of their own descendants from getting very far in conventional schemes of education. Two of Aaron Tarkington's children were so far from being dyslexic, in fact, as to themselves write books, which I have read only now, and which nobody, probably, will ever read again. Aaron's only son, Elias, wrote a technical account of the construction of the Onondaga Canal, which connected the northern end of Lake Mohiga to the Erie Canal just south of Rochester. And the youngest daughter, Felicia, wrote a novel called *Carpathia,* about a headstrong, high-born young woman in the Mohiga Valley who fell in love with a half-Indian lock-tender on that same canal.

That canal is all filled in and paved over now, and is Route 53, which forks at the head of the lake, where the locks used to be. One fork leads southwest through farm country to Scipio. The other leads southeast through the perpetual gloom of the Iroquois National Forest to the bald hilltop crowned by the battlements of the New York State Maximum Security Adult Correctional Institution at Athena, a hamlet directly across the lake from Scipio.

Bear with me. This is history. I am trying to explain how this valley, this verdant cul-de-sac, got to be what it is today.

All 3 of Aaron Tarkington's daughters married into prosperous and enterprising families in Cleveland, New York, and Wilmington, Delaware—innocently making the threat of dyslexia pandemic in an emerging ruling class of bankers and industrialists, largely displaced in my time by Germans, Koreans, Italians, English, and, of course, Japanese.

The son of Aaron, Elias, remained in Scipio and took over his father's properties, adding to them a brewery and a steam-driven carpet factory, the first such in the state. There was no water power in Scipio, whose industrial prosperity until the introduction of steam was based not on cheap energy and locally available raw materials but on inventiveness and high standards of workmanship.

Elias Tarkington never married. He was severely wounded at the age of 54 while a civilian observer at the Battle of Gettysburg, top hat and all. He was there to see the debuts of 2 of his inventions, a mobile field kitchen and a pneumatic recoil mechanism for heavy artillery. The field kitchen, incidentally, with slight modifications, would later be adopted by the Barnum &

Bailey Circus, and then by the German Army during
World War I.

Elias Tarkington was a tall and skinny man with chin
whiskers and a stovepipe hat. He was shot through the
right chest at Gettysburg, but not fatally.

The man who shot him was 1 of the few Confederate
soldiers to reach the Union lines during Pickett's
Charge. That Johnny Reb died in ecstasy among his
enemies, believing that he had shot Abraham Lincoln.
A crumbling newspaper account I have found here in
what used to be the college library, which is now the
prison library, gives his last words as follows: "Go
home, Bluebellies. Old Satan's daid."

During my 3 years in Vietnam, I certainly heard
plenty of last words by dying American footsoldiers.
Not 1 of them, however, had illusions that he had somehow accomplished something worthwhile in the process
of making the Supreme Sacrifice.

One boy of only 18 said to me while he was dying and
I was holding him in my arms, "Dirty joke, dirty joke."

3

Elias Tarkington, the severely wounded Abraham Lincoln look-alike, was brought home in 1 of his own wagons to Scipio, to his estate overlooking the town and lake.

He was not well educated, and was more a mechanic than a scientist, and so spent his last 3 years trying to invent what anyone familiar with Newton's Laws would have known was an impossibility, a perpetual-motion machine. He had no fewer than 27 contraptions built, which he foolishly expected to go on running, after he had given them an initial spin or whack, until Judgment Day.

I found 19 of those stubborn, mocking machines in the attic of what used to be their inventor's mansion, which in my time was the home of the College President, about a year after I came to work at Tarkington. I brought them back downstairs and into the 20th Century. Some of my students and I cleaned them up and restored any parts that had deteriorated during the intervening 100 years. At the least they were exquisite

13

jewelry, with garnets and amethysts for bearings, with arms and legs of exotic woods, with tumbling balls of ivory, with chutes and counterweights of silver. It was as though dying Elias hoped to overwhelm science with the magic of precious materials.

The longest my students and I could get the best of them to run was 51 seconds. Some eternity!

To me, and I passed this on to my students, the restored devices demonstrated not only how quickly anything on Earth runs down without steady infusions of energy. They reminded us, too, of the craftsmanship no longer practiced in the town below. Nobody down there in our time could make things that cunning and beautiful.

Yes, and we took the 10 machines we agreed were the most beguiling, and we put them on permanent exhibit in the foyer of this library underneath a sign whose words can surely be applied to this whole ruined planet nowadays:

THE COMPLICATED FUTILITY OF IGNORANCE

I have discovered from reading old newspapers and letters and diaries from back then that the men who built the machines for Elias Tarkington knew from the first that they would never work, whatever the reason. Yet what love they lavished on the materials that comprised them! How is this for a definition of high art: "Making the most of the raw materials of futility"?

Still another perpetual-motion machine envisioned by Elias Tarkington was what his Last Will and Testament called "The Mohiga Valley Free Institute." Upon his death, this new school would take possession of his 3,000-hectare estate above Scipio, plus half the shares in the wagon company, the carpet company, and the brewery. The other half was already owned by his sisters far away. On his deathbed he predicted that Scipio would 1 day be a great metropolis and that its wealth would transform his little college into a university to rival Harvard and Oxford and Heidelberg.

It was to offer a free college education to persons of either sex, and of any age or race or religion, living within 40 miles of Scipio. Those from farther away would pay a modest fee. In the beginning, it would have only 1 full-time employee, the President. The teachers would be recruited right here in Scipio. They would take a few hours off from work each week, to teach what they knew. The chief engineer at the wagon company, for example, whose name was André Lutz, was a native of Liège, Belgium, and had served as an apprentice to a bell founder there. He would teach Chemistry. His French wife would teach French and Watercolor Painting. The brewmaster at the brewery, Hermann Shultz, a native of Leipzig, would teach Botany and German and the flute. The Episcopalian priest, Dr. Alan Clewes, a graduate of Harvard, would teach Latin, Greek, Hebrew, and the Bible. The dying man's physician, Dalton Polk, would teach Biology and Shakespeare, and so on.

And it came to pass.

In 1869 the new college enrolled its first class, 9 students in all, and all from right here in Scipio. Four were of ordinary college age. One was a Union veteran who had lost his legs at Shiloh. One was a former black slave 40 years old. One was a spinster 82 years old.

The first President was only 26 years old, a school-teacher from Athena, 2 kilometers by water from Scipio. There was no prison over there back then, but only a slate quarry and a sawmill and a few subsistence farms. His name was John Peck. He was a cousin of the Tarkingtons'. His branch of the family, however, was and remains unhampered by dyslexia. He has numerous descendants in the present day, 1 of whom, in fact, is a speech writer for the Vice-President of the United States.

Young John Peck and his wife and 2 children and his mother-in-law arrived at Scipio by rowboat, with Peck and his wife at the oars, their children seated in the stern, and their luggage and the mother-in-law in another boat they towed behind.

They took up residence on the third floor of what had been Elias Tarkington's mansion. The rooms on the first 2 floors would be classrooms, a library, which was already a library with 280 volumes collected by the Tarkingtons, study halls, and a dining room. Many treasures from the past were taken up to the attic to make room for the new activities. Among these were the failed perpetual-motion machines. They would gather dust and cobwebs until 1978, when I found them up there, and realized what they were, and brought them down the stairs again.

One week before the first class was held, which was in Latin, taught by the Episcopalian priest Alan Clewes, André Lutz the Belgian arrived at the mansion with 3 wagons carrying a very heavy cargo, a carillon consisting of 32 bells. He had cast them on his own time and at his own expense in the wagon factory's foundry. They were made from mingled Union and Confederate rifle barrels and cannonballs and bayonets gathered up after the Battle of Gettysburg. They were the first bells and surely the last bells ever to be cast in Scipio.

Nothing, in my opinion, will ever again be cast in Scipio. No industrial arts of any sort will ever again be practiced here.

André Lutz gave the new college all those bells, even though there was no place to hang them. He said he did it because he was so sure that it would 1 day be a great university with a bell tower and everything. He was dying of emphysema as a result of the fumes from molten metals that he had been breathing since he was 10 years old. He had no time to wait for a place to hang the most wonderful consequence of his having been alive for a little while, which was all those bells, bells, bells.

They were no surprise. They had been 18 months in the making. The founders whose work he supervised had shared his dreams of immortality as they made things as impractical and beautiful as bells, bells, bells.

So all the bells but 1 from a middle octave were slathered with grease to prevent their rusting and stored in 4 ranks in the estate's great barn, 200 meters from the mansion. The 1 bell that was going to get to sing at once was installed in the cupola of the mansion, with its rope running all the way down to the first floor. It would call people to classes and, if need be, also serve as a fire alarm.

The rest of the bells, it turned out, would slumber in the loft for 30 years, until 1899, when they were hanged as a family, the 1 from the cupola included, on axles in the belfry of the tower of a splendid library given to the school by the Moellenkamp family of Cleveland.

The Moellenkamps were also Tarkingtons, since the

founder of their fortune had married a daughter of the illiterate Aaron Tarkington. Eleven of them so far had been dyslexic, and they had all gone to college in Scipio, since no other institution of higher learning would take them in.

The first Moellenkamp to graduate from here was Henry, who enrolled in 1875, when he was 19, and when the school was only 6 years old. It was at that time that its name was changed to Tarkington College. I have found the crumbling minutes of the Board of Trustees meeting at which that name change was made. Three of the 6 trustees were men who had married daughters of Aaron Tarkington, 1 of them the grandfather of Henry Moellenkamp. The other 3 trustees were the Mayor of Scipio, and a lawyer who looked after the Tarkington daughters' interests in the valley, and the area Congressman, who was surely the sisters' faithful servant, too, since they were partners with the college in his district's most important industries.

And according to the minutes, which fell apart in my hands as I read them, it was the grandfather of young Henry Moellenkamp who proposed the name change, saying that "The Mohiga Valley Free Institute" sounded too much like a poorhouse or a hospital. It is my guess that he would not have minded having the place sound like a catchment for the poor, if only he had not suffered the misfortune of having his own grandson go there.

It was in that same year, 1875, that work began across the lake from Scipio, on a hilltop above Athena, on a prison camp for young criminals from big-city slums. It was believed that fresh air and the wonders of

Nature would improve their souls and bodies to the point that they would find it natural to be good citizens.

When I came to work at Tarkington, there were only 300 students, a number that hadn't changed for 50 years. But the rustic work-camp across the lake had become a brutal fortress of iron and masonry on a naked hilltop, the New York State Maximum Security Adult Correctional Institution at Athena, keeping 5,000 of the state's worst criminals under lock and key.

Two years ago, Tarkington still had only 300 students, but the population of the prison, under hideously overcrowded conditions, had grown to 10,000. And then, 1 cold winter's night, it became the scene of the biggest prison break in American history. Until then, nobody had ever escaped from Athena.

Suddenly, everybody was free to leave, and to take a weapon from the prison armory, too, if he had use for 1. The lake between the prison and the little college was frozen solid, as easily traversed as the parking lot of a great shopping mall.

What next?

Yes, and by the time André Lutz's bells were at last made to sing as a carillon, Tarkington College had not only a new library but luxurious dormitories, a science building, an art building, a chapel, a theater, a dining hall, an administration building, 2 new buildings of classrooms, and athletic facilities that were the envy of the institutions with which it had begun to compete in track and fencing and swimming and baseball, which were Hobart, the University of Rochester, Cornell, Union, Amherst, and Bucknell.

These structures bore the names of wealthy families

as grateful as the Moellenkamps for all the college had
managed to do for offspring of theirs whom conventional colleges had deemed ineducable. Most were unrelated to the Moellenkamps or to anyone who carried
the Tarkington gene of dyslexia. Nor were the young
they sent to Tarkington necessarily troubled by dyslexia. All sorts of different things were wrong with them,
including an inability to write legibly with pen and ink,
although what they tried to write down made perfect
sense, and stammering so severe as to prevent their
saying a word in class, and petit mal, which caused their
minds to go perfectly blank for seconds or minutes
anywhere, anytime, and so on.

It was simply the Moellenkamps who first challenged
the new little college to do what it could for a seemingly
hopeless case of plutocratic juvenile incapacity, namely
Henry. Not only would Henry graduate with honors
from Tarkington. He would go on to Oxford, taking
with him a male companion who read aloud to him and
wrote down thoughts Henry could only express orally.
Henry would become 1 of the most brilliant speakers in
a golden age of American purple, bow-wow oratory,
and serve as a Congressman and then a United States
Senator from Ohio for 36 years.

That same Henry Moellenkamp was author of the
lyrics to one of the most popular turn-of-the-century
ballads, "Mary, Mary, Where Have You Gone?"

The melody of that ballad was composed by Henry's
friend Paul Dresser, brother of the novelist Theodore
Dreiser. This was 1 of the rare instances in which
Dresser set another man's words to music instead of his
own. And then Henry appropriated that tune and

wrote, or rather dictated, new words which sentimental-
ized student life in this valley.

Thus was "Mary, Mary, Where Have You Gone?"
transmogrified into the alma mater of this campus until
it became a penitentiary 2 years ago.

History.

Accident after accident has made Tarkington what it
is today. Who would dare to predict what it will be in
2021, only 20 years from now? The 2 prime movers in
the Universe are Time and Luck.

As the tag line of my favorite dirty joke would have
it: "Keep your hat on. We could wind up miles from
here."

If Henry Moellenkamp had not come out of his
mother's womb dyslexic, Tarkington College wouldn't
even have been called Tarkington College. It would
have gone on being The Mohiga Valley Free Institute,
which would have died right along with the wagon factory and the carpet factory and the brewery when the
railroads and highways connecting the East and West
were built far to the north and south of Scipio—so as
not to bridge the lake, so as not to have to penetrate the
deep and dark virgin hardwood forest, now the Iroquois National Forest, to the east and south of here.

If Henry Moellenkamp hadn't come out of his
mother's womb dyslexic, and if that mother hadn't been
a Tarkington and so known about the little college on
Lake Mohiga, this library would never have been built
and filled with 800,000 bound volumes. When I was a
professor here, that was 70,000 more bound volumes
than Swarthmore College had! Among small colleges,

this library used to be second only to the 1 at Oberlin, which had 1,000,000 bound volumes.

So what is this structure in which I sit now, thanks to Time and Luck? It is nothing less, friends and neighbors, than the greatest prison library in the history of crime and punishment!

It is very lonely in here. Hello? Hello?

I might have said the same sort of thing back when this was an 800,000-bound-volume college library: "It is very lonely in here. Hello? Hello?"

I have just looked up Harvard University. It has 13,000,000 bound volumes now. What a read!

And almost every book written for or about the ruling class.

If Henry Moellenkamp hadn't come out of his mother's womb dyslexic, there would never have been a tower in which to hang the Lutz Carillon.

Those bells might never have gotten to reverberate in the valley or anywhere. They probably would have been melted up and made back into weapons during World War I.

If Henry Moellenkamp had not come out of his mother's womb dyslexic, these heights above Scipio might have been all darkness on the cold winter night 2 years ago, with Lake Mohiga frozen hard as a parking lot, when 10,000 prisoners at Athena were suddenly set free.

Instead, there was a little galaxy of beckoning lights up here.

4

Regardless of whether Henry Moellenkamp came out of his mother's womb dyslexic or not, I was born in Wilmington, Delaware, 18 months before this country joined the fighting in World War II. I have not seen Wilmington since. That is where they keep my birth certificate. I was the only child of a housewife and, as I've said, a chemical engineer. My father was then employed by E. I. Du Pont de Nemours & Company, a manufacturer of high explosives, among other things.

When I was 2 years old, we moved to Midland City, Ohio, where a washing-machine company named Robo-Magic Corporation was beginning to make bomb-release mechanisms and swivel mounts for machine guns on B-17 bombers. The plastics industry was then in its infancy, and Father was sent to Robo-Magic to determine what synthetic materials from Du Pont could be used in the weapons systems in place of metal, in order to make them lighter.

By the time the war was over, the company had gotten out of the washing-machine business entirely, had changed its name to Barrytron, Limited, and was making weapon, airplane, and motor vehicle parts composed of plastics it had developed on its own. My father had become the company's Vice-President in Charge of Research and Development.

When I was about 17, Du Pont bought Barrytron in order to capture several of its patents. One of the plastics Father had helped to develop, I remember, had the ability to scatter radar signals, so that an airplane clad in it would look like a flock of geese to our enemies.

This material, which has since been used to make virtually indestructible skateboards and crash helmets and skis and motorcycle fenders and so on, was an excuse, when I was a boy, for increasing security precautions at Barrytron. To keep Communists from finding out how it was made, a single fence topped with barbed wire was no longer adequate. A second fence was put outside that one, and the space between them was patrolled around the clock by humorless, jackbooted armed guards with lean and hungry Dobermans.

When Du Pont took over Barrytron, the double fence, the Dobermans, my father and all, I was a high school senior, all set to go to the University of Michigan to learn how to be a journalist, to serve John Q. Public's right to know. Two members of my 6-piece band, The Soul Merchants, the clarinet and the string bass, were also going to Michigan.

We were going to stick together and go on making music at Ann Arbor. Who knows? We might have become so popular that we went on world tours and made great fortunes, and been superstars at peace rallies and love-ins when the Vietnam War came along.

Cadets at West Point did not make music. The musicians in the dance band and the marching band were Regular Army enlisted men, members of the servant class.

They were under orders to play music as written, note for note, and never mind how they felt about the music or about anything.

For that matter, there wasn't any student publication at West Point. So never mind how the cadets felt about anything. Not interesting.

I was fine, but all kinds of things were going wrong with my father's life. Du Pont was looking him over, as they were looking over everybody at Barrytron, deciding whether to keep him on or not. He was also having a love affair with a married woman whose husband caught him in the act and beat him up.

This was a sensitive subject with my parents, naturally, so I never discussed it with them. But the story was all over town, and Father had a black eye. He didn't play any sports, so he had to make up a story about falling down the basement stairs. Mother weighed about 90 kilograms by then, and berated him all the time about his having sold all his Barrytron stock 2 years too soon. If he had hung on to it until the Du Pont takeover, he would have had $1,000,000, back when it meant something to be a millionaire. If I had been learning-disabled, he could easily have afforded to send me to Tarkington.

Unlike me, he was the sort of man who had to be in

extremis in order to commit adultery. According to a story I heard from enemies at high school, Father had done the jumping-out-the-window thing, hippity-hopping like Peter Cottontail across backyards with his pants around his ankles, and getting bitten by a dog, and getting tangled up in a clothesline, and all the rest of it. That could have been an exaggeration. I never asked.

I myself was deeply troubled by our little family's image problem, which was complicated when Mother broke her nose 2 days after Father got the black eye. To the outside world it looked as though she had said something to Father about the reason he had a black eye, and his reply had been to slug her. I didn't think he would ever slug her, no matter what.

There is a not quite remote possibility that he really did slug her, of course. Lesser men would have slugged her under similar circumstances. The real truth of the matter became unavailable to historians forever when the falling ceiling of a gift shop on the Canadian side of Niagara Falls killed both participants, as I've said, some 20 years ago. They were said to have died instantly. They never knew what hit them, which is the best way to go.

There was no argument about that in Vietnam or, I suppose, on any battlefield. One kid I remember stepped on an antipersonnel mine. The mine could have been one of our own. His best friend from Basic Training asked him what he could do for him, and the kid replied: "Turn me off like a light bulb, Sam."

The dying kid was white. The kid who wanted to help him was black, or a light tan, actually. His features were practically white, you would have to say.

A woman I was making love to a few years ago asked me if my parents were still alive. She wanted to know more about me, now that we had our clothes off.

I told her that they had suffered violent deaths in a foreign country, which was true. Canada is a foreign country.

But then I heard myself spinning this fantastic tale of their being on a safari in Tanganyika, a place about which I know almost nothing. I told that woman, and she believed me, that my parents and their guide were shot by poachers who were killing elephants for their ivory and mistook them for game wardens. I said that the poachers put their bodies on top of anthills, so that their skeletons were soon picked clean. They could be positively identified only by their dental work.

I used to find it easy and even exhilarating to lie that elaborately. I don't anymore. And I wonder now if I didn't develop that unwholesome habit very young, and because my parents were such an embarrassment, and especially my mother, who was fat enough to be a circus freak. I described much more attractive parents than I really had, in order to make people who knew nothing about them think well of me.

And during my final year in Vietnam, when I was in Public Information, I found it as natural as breathing to tell the press and replacements fresh off the boats or planes that we were clearly winning, and that the folks back home should be proud and happy about all the good things we were doing there.

I learned to lie like that in high school.

Another thing I learned in high school that was helpful in Vietnam: Alcohol and marijuana, if used in moderation, plus loud, usually low-class music, make stress and boredom infinitely more bearable. It was manna from Heaven that I came into this world with a gift for moderation in my intake of mood-modifying substances. During my last 2 years in high school, I don't think my parents even suspected that I was half in the bag a lot of the time. All they ever complained about was the music, when I played the radio or the phonograph or when The Soul Merchants rehearsed in our basement, which Mom and Dad said was jungle music, and much too loud.

In Vietnam, the music was always much too loud. Practically everybody was half in the bag, including Chaplains. Several of the most gruesome accidents I had to explain to the press during my last year over there were caused by people who had rendered themselves imbecilic or maniacal by ingesting too much of what, if taken in moderation, could be a helpful chemical. I ascribed all such accidents, of course, to human error. The press understood. Who on this Earth hasn't made a mistake or 2?

The assassination of an Austrian archduke led to World War I, and probably to World War II as well. Just as surely, my father's black eye brought me to the sorry state in which I find myself today. He was looking for some way, almost any way, to recapture the respect of the community, and to attract favorable attention from Barrytron's new owner, Du Pont. Du Pont, of course, has now been taken over by I. G. Farben of Germany, the same company that manufactured and packaged and labeled and addressed the cyanide gas used to kill civilians of all ages, including babes in arms, during the Holocaust.

What a planet.

So Father, his injured eye looking like a slit in a purple and yellow omelet, asked me if I was likely to receive any sort of honors at high school graduation. He didn't say so, but he was frantic for something to brag about at work. He was so desperate that he was trying to get blood out of the turnip of my nonparticipation in high school sports, student government, or school-sponsored extracurricular activities. My grade average was high enough to get me into the University of Michigan, and on the honor roll now and then, but not into the National Honor Society.

It was so pitiful! It made me mad, too, because he was trying to make me partly responsible for the family's image problem, which was all his fault. "I was always sorry you didn't go out for football," he said, as though a touchdown would have made everything all right again.

"Too late now," I said.

"You let those 4 years slip by without doing anything but making jungle music," he said.

It occurs to me now, a mere 43 years later, that I might have said to him that at least I managed my sex life better than he had managed his. I was getting laid all the time, thanks to jungle music, and so were the other Soul Merchants. Certain sorts of not just girls but full-grown women, too, found us glamorous free spirits up on the bandstand, imitating black people and smoking marijuana, and loving ourselves when we made music, and laughing about God knows what just about anytime.

I guess my love life is over now. Even if I could get out of prison, I wouldn't want to give some trusting

woman tuberculosis. She would be scared to death of
getting AIDS, and I would give her TB instead.
Wouldn't that be nice?

So now I will have to make do with memories. As a
prosthesis for my memory, I have begun to list all the
women, excluding my wife and prostitutes, with whom
I have "gone all the way," as we used to say in high
school. I find it impossible to remember any conquest I
made as a teenager with clarity, to separate fact from
fantasy. It was all a dream. So I begin my list with
Shirley Kern, to whom I made love when I was 20.
Shirley is my datum.

How many names will there be on the list? Too early
to tell, but wouldn't that number, whatever it turns out
to be, be as good a thing as any to put on my tombstone
as an enigmatic epitaph?

I am certainly sorry if I ruined the lives of any of
those women who believed me when I said I loved them.
I can only hope against hope that Shirley Kern and all
the rest of them are still OK.

If it is any consolation to those who may not be OK,
my own life was ruined by a Science Fair.

Father asked me if there wasn't some school-sponsored extracurricular activity I could still try out for.
This was only 8 weeks before my graduation! So I said,
in a spirit of irony, since he knew science did not delight
me as it delighted him, that my last opportunity to
amount to anything was the County Science Fair. I got
Bs in Physics and Chemistry, but you could stuff both
those subjects up your fundament as far as I was concerned.

But Father rose from his chair in a state of sick

excitement. "Let's go down in the basement," he said. "There's work to do."

"What kind of work?" I said. This was about midnight.

And he said, "You are going to enter and win the Science Fair."

Which I did. Or, rather, Father entered and won the Science Fair, requiring only that I sign an affidavit swearing that the exhibit was all my own work, and that I memorize his explanation of what it proved. It was about crystals and how they grew and why they grew.

His competition was weak. He was, after all, a 43-year-old chemical engineer with 20 years in industry, taking on teenagers in a community where few parents had higher educations. The main business in the county back then was still agriculture, corn and pigs and beef cattle. Barrytron was the sole sophisticated industry, and only a handful of people such as Father understood its processes and apparatus. Most of the company's employees were content to do what they were told and incurious as to how it was, exactly, that they had worked the miracles that somehow arrived all packaged and labeled and addressed on the loading docks.

I am reminded now of dead American soldiers, teenagers mostly, all packaged and labeled and addressed on loading docks in Vietnam. How many people knew or cared how these curious artifacts were actually manufactured?

A few.

Why Father and I were not branded as swindlers, why my exhibit was not thrown out of the Science Fair, why I am a prisoner awaiting trial now instead of a star reporter for the Korean owners of *The New York Times* has to do with compassion, I now believe. The feeling was general in the community, I think, that our little family had suffered enough. Nobody in the county gave much of a darn about science anyway.

The other exhibits were so dumb and pitiful, too, that the best of them would make the county look stupid if it and its honest creator went on to the statewide competition in Cleveland. Our exhibit sure looked slick and tidy. Another big plus from the judges' point of view, maybe, when they thought about what the county's best was going to be up against in Cleveland: our exhibit was extremely hard for an ordinary person to understand or find at all interesting.

I remained philosophical, thanks to marijuana and alcohol, while the community decided whether to crucify me as a fraud or to crown me as a genius. Father may have had a buzz on, too. Sometimes it's hard to tell. I served under 2 Generals in Vietnam who drank a quart of whiskey a day, but it was hard to detect. They always looked serious and dignified.

So off Father and I went to Cleveland. His spirits were high. I knew we would go smash up there. I don't know why he didn't know we would go smash up there. The only advice he gave me was to keep my shoulders back when I was explaining my exhibit and not to smoke where the judges might see me doing it. He was talking about ordinary cigarettes. He didn't know I smoked the other kind.

I make no apologies for having been zapped during my darkest days in high school. Winston Churchill was bombed out of his skull on brandy and Cuban cigars during the darkest days of World War II.

Hitler, of course, thanks to the advanced technology of Germany, was among the first human beings to turn their brains to cobwebs with amphetamine. He actually chewed on carpets, they say. Yum yum.

Mother did not come to Cleveland with Father and me. She was ashamed to leave the house, she was so big and fat. So I had to do most of the marketing after school. I also had to do most of the housework, she had so much trouble getting around. My familiarity with housework was useful at West Point, and then again when my mother-in-law and then my wife went nuts. It was actually sort of relaxing, because I could see that I had accomplished something undeniably good, and I didn't have to think about my troubles while I was doing it. How my mother's eyes used to shine when she saw what I had cooked for her!

My mother's story is 1 of the few real success stories in this book. She joined Weight Watchers when she was 60, which is my age now. When the ceiling fell on her at Niagara Falls, she weighed only 52 kilograms!

This library is full of stories of supposed triumphs, which makes me very suspicious of it. It's misleading for people to read about great successes, since even for middle-class and upper-class white people, in my experience, failure is the norm. It is unfair to youngsters particularly to leave them wholly unprepared for monster screw-ups and starring roles in Keystone Kop comedies and much, much worse.

The Ohio Science Fair took place in Cleveland's beautiful Moellenkamp Auditorium. The theater seats had been removed and replaced with tables for all the exhibits. There was a hint of my then distant future in the auditorium's having been given to the city by the Moellenkamps, the same coal and shipping family that gave Tarkington College this library. This was long before they sold the boats and mines to a British and Omani consortium based in Luxembourg.

But the present was bad enough. Even as Father and I were setting up our exhibit, we were spotted by other contestants as a couple of comedians, as Laurel and Hardy, maybe, with Father as the fat and officious one and me as the dumb and skinny one. The thing was, Father was doing all the setting up, and I was standing around looking bored. All I wanted to do was go outside and hide behind a tree or something and smoke a cigarette. We were violating the most basic rule of the Fair, which was that the young exhibitors were supposed to do all the work, from start to finish. Parents or teachers or whatever were forbidden in writing to help at all.

It was as though I had entered the Soapbox Derby over in Akron, Ohio, in a car for coasting down hills that I had supposedly built myself but was actually my dad's Ferrari Gran Turismo.

We hadn't made any of the exhibit in the basement. When, at the very beginning, Father said that we should go down in the basement and get to work, we had actually gone down in the basement. But we stayed down there for only about 10 minutes while he thought and thought, growing ever more excited. I didn't say anything.

Actually, I *did* say one thing. "Mind if I smoke?" I said.

"Go right ahead," he said.

That was a breakthrough for me. It meant I could smoke in the house whenever I pleased, and he wouldn't say anything.

Then he led the way back up to the living room. He sat down at Mother's desk and made a list of things that should go into the exhibit.

"What are you doing, Dad?" I said.

"Shh," he said. "I'm busy. Don't bother me."

So I didn't bother him. I had more than enough to think about as it was. I was pretty sure I had gonorrhea. It was some sort of urethral infection, which was making me very uncomfortable. But I hadn't seen a doctor about it, because the doctor, by law, would have had to report me to the Department of Health, and my parents would have been told about it, as though they hadn't had enough heartaches already.

Whatever the infection was, it cleared itself up without my doing anything about it. It couldn't have been gonorrhea, which never stops eating you up of its own accord. Why should it ever stop of its own accord? It's having such a nice time. Why call off the party? Look how healthy and happy the kids are.

Twice in later life I would contract what was unambiguously gonorrhea, once in Tegucigalpa, Honduras, and then again in Saigon, now Ho Chi Minh City, in Vietnam. In both instances I told the doctors about the self-healing infection I had had in high school.

It might have been yeast, they said. I should have opened a bakery.

So Father started coming home from work with pieces of the exhibit, which had been made to his order at Barrytron: pedestals and display cases, and explanatory signs and labels made by the print shop that did a lot of work for Barrytron. The crystals themselves came from a Pittsburgh chemical supply house that did a lot of business with Barrytron. One crystal, I remember, came all the way from Burma.

The chemical supply house must have gone to some trouble to get together a remarkable collection of crystals for us, since what they sent us couldn't have come from their regular stock. In order to please a big customer like Barrytron, they may have gone to somebody who collected and sold crystals for their beauty and rarity, not as chemicals but as jewelry.

At any rate, the crystals, which were of museum quality, caused Father to utter these famous last words after he spread them out on the coffee table in our living room, gloatingly: "Son, there is no way we can lose."

Well, as Jean-Paul Sartre says in Bartlett's *Familiar Quotations,* "Hell is other people." Other people made short work of Father's and my invincible contest entry in Cleveland 43 years ago.

Generals George Armstrong Custer at the Little Bighorn, and Robert E. Lee at Gettysburg, and William Westmoreland in Vietnam all come to mind.

Somebody said 1 time, I remember, that General Custer's famous last words were, "Where are all these blankety-blank Injuns comin' from?"

Father and I, and not our pretty crystals, were for a little while the most fascinating exhibit in Moellenkamp Auditorium. We were a demonstration of abnormal psychology. Other contestants and their mentors gathered around us and put us through our paces. They certainly knew which buttons to push, so to speak, to make us change color or twist and turn or grin horribly or whatever.

One contestant asked Father how old he was and what high school he was attending.

That was when we should have packed up our things and gotten out of there. The judges hadn't had a look at us yet, and neither had any reporters. We hadn't yet put up the sign that said what my name was and what school system I represented. We hadn't yet said anything worth remembering.

If we had folded up and vanished quietly right then and there, leaving nothing but an empty table, we might have entered the history of American science as no-shows who got sick or something. There was already an empty table, which would stay empty, only 5 meters away from ours. Father and I had heard that it was going to stay empty and why. The would-be exhibitor and his mother and father were all in the hospital in Lima, Ohio, not Lima, Peru. That was their hometown. They had scarcely backed out of their driveway the day before, headed for Cleveland, they thought, with the exhibit in the trunk, when they were rear-ended by a drunk driver.

The accident wouldn't have been half as serious as it turned out to be if the exhibit hadn't included several bottles of different acids which broke and touched off the gasoline. Both vehicles were immediately engulfed in flames.

The exhibit was, I think, meant to show several important services that acids, which most people were afraid of and didn't like to think much about, were performing every day for Humanity.

The people who looked us over and asked us questions, and did not like what they saw and heard, sent for a judge. They wanted us disqualified. We were worse than dishonest. We were ridiculous!

I wanted to throw up. I said to Father, "Dad, honest to God, I think we better get out of here. We made a mistake."

But he said we had nothing to be ashamed of, and that we certainly weren't going to go home with our tails between our legs.

Vietnam!

So a judge did come over, and easily determined that I had no understanding whatsoever of the exhibit. He then took Father aside and negotiated a political settlement, man to man. He did not want to stir up bad feelings in our home county, which had sent me to Cleveland as its champion. Nor did he want to humiliate Father, who was an upstanding member of his community who obviously had not read the rules carefully. He would not humiliate us with a formal disqualification, which might attract unfavorable publicity, if Father in turn would not insist on having my entry put in serious competition with the rest as though it were legitimate.

When the time came, he said, he and the other judges would simply pass us by without comment. It would be their secret that we couldn't possibly win anything.

That was the deal.

History.

5

The person who won that year was a girl from Cincinnati. As it happened, she too had an exhibit about crystallography. She, however, had either grown her own or gathered specimens herself from creek beds and caves and coal mines within 100 kilometers of her home. Her name was Mary Alice French, I remember, and she would go on to place very close to the bottom in the National Finals in Washington, D.C.

When she set off for the Finals, I heard, Cincinnati was so proud of her and so sure she would win, or at least place very high with her crystals, that the Mayor declared "Mary Alice French Day."

I have to wonder now, with so much time in which to think about people I've hurt, if Father and I didn't indirectly help set up Mary Alice French for her terrible disappointment in Washington. There is a good chance that the judges in Cleveland gave her First Prize because of the moral contrast between her exhibit and ours.

Perhaps, during the judging, science was given a

backseat, and because of our ill fame, she represented a golden opportunity to teach a rule superior to any law of science: that honesty was the best policy.

But who knows?

Many, many years after Mary Alice French had her heart broken in Washington, and I had become a teacher at Tarkington, I had a male student from Cincinnati, Mary Alice French's hometown. His mother's side of the family had just sold Cincinnati's sole remaining daily paper and its leading TV station, and a lot of radio stations and weekly papers, too, to the Sultan of Brunei, reputedly the richest individual on Earth.

This student looked about 12 when he came to us. He was actually 21, but his voice had never changed, and he was only 150 centimeters tall. As a result of the sale to the Sultan, he personally was said to be worth $30,000,000, but he was scared to death of his own shadow.

He could read and write and do math all the way up through algebra and trigonometry, which he had taught himself. He was also probably the best chess player in the history of the college. But he had no social graces, and probably never would have any, because he found everything about life so frightening.

I asked him if he had ever heard of a woman about my age in Cincinnati whose name was Mary Alice French.

He replied: "I don't know anybody or anything. Please don't ever talk to me again. Tell everybody to stop talking to me."

I never did find out what he did with all his money, if anything. Somebody said he got married. Hard to believe!

Some fortune hunter must have got him.
Smart girl. She must be on Easy Street.

But to get back to the Science Fair in Cleveland: I headed for the nearest exit after Father and the judge made their deal. I needed fresh air. I needed a whole new planet or death. Anything would be better than what I had.

The exit was blocked by a spectacularly dressed man. He was wholly unlike anyone else in the auditorium. He was, incredibly, what I myself would become: a Lieutenant Colonel in the Regular Army, with many rows of ribbons on his chest. He was in full-dress uniform, with a gold citation cord and paratrooper's wings and boots. We were not then at war anywhere, so the sight of a military man all dolled up like that among civilians, especially so early in the day, was startling. He had been sent there to recruit budding young scientists for his alma mater, the United States Military Academy at West Point.

The Academy had been founded soon after the Revolutionary War because the country had so few military officers with mathematical and engineering skills essential to victories in what was modern warfare way back then, mainly mapmaking and cannonballs. Now, with radar and rockets and airplanes and nuclear weapons and all the rest of it, the same problem had come up again.

And there I was in Cleveland, with a great big round badge pinned over my heart like a target, which said:

EXHIBITOR.

This Lieutenant Colonel, whose name was Sam Wakefield, would not only get me into West Point. In Vietnam, where he was a Major General, he would award me a Silver Star for extraordinary valor and gallantry. He would retire from the Army when the war still had a year to go, and become President of Tarkington College, now Tarkington Prison. And when I myself got out of the Army, he would hire me to teach Physics and play the bells, bells, bells.

Here are the first words Sam Wakefield ever spoke to me, when I was 18 and he was 36:

"What's the hurry, Son?"

6

"What's the hurry, Son?" he said. And then, "If you've got a minute, I'd like to talk to you." So I stopped. That was the biggest mistake of my life. There were plenty of other exits, and I should have headed for 1 of those. At that moment, every other exit led to the University of Michigan and journalism and music-making, and a lifetime of saying and wearing what I goshdarned pleased. Any other exit, in all probability, would have led me to a wife who wouldn't go insane on me, and kids who gave me love and respect.

Any other exit would have led to a certain amount of misery, I know, life being what it is. But I don't think it would have led me to Vietnam, and then to teaching the unteachable at Tarkington College, and then getting fired by Tarkington, and then teaching the unteachable at the penitentiary across the lake until the biggest prison break in American history. And now I myself am a prisoner.

43

But I stopped before the 1 exit blocked by Sam Wakefield.

There went the ball game.

Sam Wakefield asked me if I had ever considered the advantages of a career in the military. This was a man who had been wounded in World War II, the 1 war I would have liked to fight in, and then in Korea. He would eventually resign from the Army with the Vietnam War still going on, and then become President of Tarkington College, and then blow his brains out.

I said I had already been accepted by the University of Michigan and had no interest in soldiering. He wasn't having any luck at all. The sort of kid who had reached a state-level Science Fair honestly wanted to go to Cal Tech or MIT, or someplace a lot friendlier to freestyle thinking than West Point. So he was desperate. He was going around the country recruiting the dregs of Science Fairs. He didn't ask me about my exhibit. He didn't ask about my grades. He wanted my body, no matter what it was.

And then Father came along, looking for me. The next thing I knew, Father and Sam Wakefield were laughing and shaking hands.

Father was happier than I had seen him in years. He said to me, "The folks back home will think that's better than any prize at a Science Fair."

"What's better?" I said.

"You have just won an appointment to the United States Military Academy," he said. "I've got a son I can be proud of now."

Seventeen years later, in 1975, I was a Lieutenant Colonel on the roof of the American Embassy in Saigon, keeping everybody but Americans off helicopters that were ferrying badly rattled people out to ships offshore. We had lost a war!

Losers!

I wasn't the worst young scientist Sam Wakefield persuaded to come to West Point. One classmate of mine, from a little high school in Wyoming, had shown early promise by making an electric chair for rats, with little straps and a little black hood and all.

That was Jack Patton. He was no relation to "Old Blood and Guts" Patton, the famous General in World War II. He became my brother-in-law. I married his sister Margaret. She came with her folks from Wyoming to see him graduate, and I fell in love with her. We sure could dance.

Jack Patton was killed by a sniper in Hué—pronounced "whay." He was a Lieutenant Colonel in the Combat Engineers. I wasn't there, but they say he got it right between the eyes. Talk about marksmanship! Whoever shot him was a real winner.

The sniper didn't stay a winner very long, though, I heard. Hardly anybody does. Some of our people figured out where he was. I heard he couldn't have been more than 15 years old. He was a boy, not a man, but if he was going to play men's games he was going to have to pay men's penalties. After they killed him, I heard, they put his little testicles and penis in his mouth as a warning to anybody else who might choose to be a sniper.

Law and order. Justice swift and justice sure.

Let me hasten to say that no unit under my command was encouraged to engage in the mutilation of bodies of enemies, nor would I have winked at it if I had heard

about it. One platoon in a battalion I led, on its own
initiative, took to leaving aces of spades on the bodies
of enemies, as sort of calling cards, I guess. This wasn't
mutilation, strictly speaking, but still I put a stop to it.

What a footsoldier can do to a body with his pip-
squeak technology is nothing, of course, when compared with the ordinary, unavoidable, perfectly routine
effects of aerial bombing and artillery. One time I saw
the severed head of a bearded old man resting on the
guts of an eviscerated water buffalo, covered with flies
in a bomb crater by a paddy in Cambodia. The plane
whose bomb made the crater was so high when it
dropped it that it couldn't even be seen from the
ground. But what its bomb did, I would have to say,
sure beat the ace of spades for a calling card.

I don't think Jack Patton would have wanted the
sniper who killed him mutilated, but you never know.
When he was alive he was like a dead man in 1 respect:
everything was pretty much all right with him.

Everything, and I mean everything, was a joke to
him, or so he said. His favorite expression right up to
the end was, "I had to laugh like hell." If Lieutenant
Colonel Patton is in Heaven, and I don't think many
truly professional soldiers have ever expected to wind
up there, at least not recently, he might at this very
moment be telling about how his life suddenly stopped
in Hué, and then adding, without even smiling, "I had
to laugh like hell." That was the thing: Patton would tell
about some supposedly serious or beautiful or dangerous or holy event during which he had had to laugh like
hell, but he hadn't really laughed. He kept a straight
face, too, when he told about it afterward. In all his life,

I don't think anybody ever heard him do what he said he had to do all the time, which was laugh like hell.

He said he had to laugh like hell when he won a science prize in high school for making an electric chair for rats, but he hadn't. A lot of people wanted him to stage a public demonstration of the chair with a tranquilized rat, wanted him to shave the head of a groggy rat and strap it to the chair, and, according to Jack, ask it if it had any last words to say, maybe wanted to express remorse for the life of crime it had led.

The execution never took place. There was enough common sense in Patton's high school, although not in the Science Department, apparently, to have such an event denounced as cruelty to dumb animals. Again, Jack Patton said without smiling, "I had to laugh like hell."

He said he had to laugh like hell when I married his sister Margaret. He said Margaret and I shouldn't take offense at that. He said he had to laugh like hell when anybody got married.

I am absolutely sure that Jack did not know that there was inheritable insanity on his mother's side of the family, and neither did his sister, who would become my bride. When I married Margaret, their mother seemed perfectly OK still, except for a mania for dancing, which was a little scary sometimes, but harmless. Dancing until she dropped wasn't nearly as loony as wanting to bomb North Vietnam back to the Stone Age, or bombing anyplace back to the Stone Age.

My mother-in-law Mildred grew up in Peru, Indiana, but never talked about Peru, even after she went crazy, except to say that Cole Porter, a composer of ultrasophisticated popular songs during the first half of the last century, was also born in Peru.

My mother-in-law ran away from Peru when she was 18, and never went back again. She worked her way through the University of Wyoming, in Laramie, of all places, which I guess was about as far away from Peru as she could get without leaving the Milky Way. That was where she met her husband, who was then a student in the university's School of Veterinary Science.

Only after the Vietnam War, with Jack long dead, did Margaret and I realize that she wanted nothing more to do with Peru because so many people there knew she came from a family famous for spawning lunatics. And then she got married, keeping her family's terrifying history to herself, and she reproduced.

My own wife married and reproduced in all innocence of the danger she herself was in, and the risk she would pass on to our children.

Our own children, having grown up with a notoriously insane grandmother in the house, fled this valley as soon as they could, just as she had fled Peru. But they haven't reproduced, and with their knowing what they do about their booby-trapped genes, I doubt that they ever will.

Jack Patton never married. He never said he wanted kids. That could be a clue that he did know about his crazy relatives in Peru, after all. But I don't believe that. He was against everybody's reproducing, since human beings were, in his own words, "about 1,000 times dumber and meaner than they think they are."

I myself, obviously, have finally come around to his point of view.

During our plebe year, I remember, Jack all of a sudden decided that he was going to be a cartoonist, although he had never thought of being that before. He was compulsive. I could imagine him back in high school in Wyoming, all of a sudden deciding to build an electric chair for rats.

The first cartoon he ever drew, and the last one, was of 2 rhinoceroses getting married. A regular human preacher in a church was saying to the congregation that anybody who knew any reason these 2 should not be joined together in holy matrimony should speak now or forever hold his peace.

This was long before I had even met his sister Margaret.

We were roommates, and would be for all 4 years. So he showed me the cartoon and said he bet he could sell it to *Playboy*.

I asked him what was funny about it. He couldn't draw for sour apples. He had to tell me that the bride and groom were rhinoceroses. I thought they were a couple of sofas maybe, or maybe a couple of smashed-up sedans. That would have been fairly funny, come to think of it: 2 smashed-up sedans taking wedding vows. They were going to settle down.

"What's funny about it?" said Jack incredulously. "Where's your sense of humor? If somebody doesn't stop the wedding, those two will mate and have a baby rhinoceros."

"Of course," I said.

"For Pete's sake," he said, "what could be uglier and dumber than a rhinoceros? Just because something can reproduce, that doesn't mean it should reproduce."

I pointed out that to a rhinoceros another rhinoceros was wonderful.

"That's the point," he said. "Every kind of animal thinks its own kind of animal is wonderful. So people getting married think they're wonderful, and that they're going to have a baby that's wonderful, when actually they're as ugly as rhinoceroses. Just because we think we're so wonderful doesn't mean we really are. We could be really terrible animals and just never admit it because it would hurt so much."

During Jack's and my cow year at the Point, I remember, which would have been our junior year at a regular college, we were ordered to walk a tour for 3 hours on the Quadrangle, in a military manner, as though on serious guard duty, in full uniform and carrying rifles. This was punishment for our having failed to report another cadet who had cheated on a final examination in Electrical Engineering. The Honor Code required not only that we never lie or cheat but that we snitch on anybody who had done those things.

We hadn't seen the cadet cheat. We hadn't even been in the same class with him. But we were with him, along with one other cadet, when he got drunk in Philadelphia after the Army–Navy game. He got so drunk he confessed that he had cheated on the exam the previous June. Jack and I told him to shut up, that we didn't want to hear about it, and that we were going to forget about it, since it probably wasn't true anyway.

But the other cadet, who would later be fragged in Vietnam, turned all of us in. We were as corrupt as the cheater, supposedly, for trying to cover up for him. "Fragging," incidentally, was a new word in the English language that came out of the Vietnam War. It meant pitching a fizzing fragmentation grenade into the sleeping quarters of an unpopular officer. I don't mean to boast, but the whole time I was in Vietnam nobody offered to frag me.

The cheater was thrown out, even though he was a firstie, which meant he would graduate in only 6 more months. And Jack and I had to walk a 3-hour tour at night and in an ice-cold rain. We weren't supposed to talk to each other or to anyone. But the nonsensical posts he and I had to march intersected at 1 point. Jack muttered to me at one such meeting, "What would you do if you heard somebody had just dropped an atom bomb on New York City?"

It would be 10 minutes before we passed again. I thought of a few answers that were obvious, such as that I would be horrified, I would want to cry, and so on. But I understood that he didn't want to hear my answer. Jack wanted me to hear his answer.

So here he came with his answer. He looked me in the eye, and he said without a flicker of a smile, "I'd laugh like hell."

The last time I heard him say that he had to laugh like hell was in Saigon, where I ran into him in a bar. He told me that he had just been awarded a Silver Star, which made him my equal, since I already had one. He had been with a platoon from his company, which was planting mines on paths leading to a village believed to be sympathetic with the enemy, when a firefight broke out. So he called for air support, and the planes dropped napalm, which is jellied gasoline developed by Harvard University, on the village, killing Vietnamese of both sexes and all ages. Afterward, he was ordered to count the bodies, and to assume that they had all been enemies, so that the number of bodies could be in the news that day. That engagement was what he got the Silver Star for. "I had to laugh like hell," he said, but he didn't crack a smile.

He would have wanted to laugh like hell if he had seen me on the roof of our embassy in Saigon with my pistol drawn. I had won my Silver Star for finding and personally killing 5 enemy soldiers who were hiding in a tunnel underground. Now I was on a rooftop, while regiments of the enemy were right out in the open, with no need to hide from anybody, taking possession without opposition of the streets below. There they were down there, in case I wanted to kill lots more of them. *Pow! Pow! Pow!*

I was up there to keep Vietnamese who had been on our side from getting onto helicopters that were ferrying Americans only, civilian employees at the embassy and their dependents, to our Navy ships offshore. The enemy could have shot down the helicopters and come up and captured or killed us, if they had wanted. But all they had ever wanted from us was that we go home. They certainly captured or killed the Vietnamese I kept off the helicopter after the very last of the Americans, who was Lieutenant Colonel Eugene Debs Hartke, was out of there.

The rest of that day:

The helicopter carrying the last American to leave Vietnam joined a swarm of helicopters over the South China Sea, driven from their roosts on land and running out of gasoline. How was that for Natural History in the 20th Century: the sky filled with chattering, man-made pterodactyls, suddenly homeless, unable to swim a stroke, about to drown or starve to death.

Below us, deployed as far as the eye could see, was the most heavily armed armada in history, in no danger whatsoever from anyone. We could have all the deep blue sea we wanted, as far as the enemy was concerned. Enjoy! Enjoy!

My own helicopter was told by radio to hover with 2 others over a minesweeper, which had a landing platform for 1 pterodactyl, its own, which took off so ours could land. Down we came, and we got out, and sailors pushed our big, dumb, clumsy bird overboard. That process was repeated twice, and then the ship's own improbable creature claimed its roost again. I had a look inside it later on. It was loaded with electronic gear that could detect mines and submarines under the water, and incoming missiles and planes in the sky above.

And then the Sun itself followed the last American helicopter to leave Saigon to the bottom of the deep blue sea.

At the age of 35, Eugene Debs Hartke was again as dissolute with respect to alcohol and marijuana and loose women as he had been during his last 2 years in high school. And he had lost all respect for himself and the leadership of his country, just as, 17 years earlier, he had lost all respect for himself and his father at the Cleveland, Ohio, Science Fair.

His mentor Sam Wakefield, the man who recruited him for West Point, had quit the Army a year earlier in order to speak out against the war. He had become President of Tarkington College through powerful family connections.

Three years after that, Sam Wakefield would commit
suicide. So there is another loser for you, even though
he had been a Major General and then a College President. I think exhaustion got him. I say that not only
because he seemed very tired all the time to me, but
because his suicide note wasn't even original and didn't
seem to have that much to do with him personally. It
was word for word the same suicide note left way back
in 1932, when I was a negative 8 years old, by another
loser, George Eastman, inventor of the Kodak camera
and founder of Eastman Kodak, now defunct, only 75
kilometers north of here.

Both notes said this and nothing more: "My work is
done."

In Sam Wakefield's case, that completed work, if he
didn't want to count the Vietnam War, consisted of 3
new buildings, which probably would have been built
anyway, no matter who was Tarkington's President.

I am not writing this book for people below the age
of 18, but I see no harm in telling young people to
prepare for failure rather than success, since failure is
the main thing that is going to happen to them.

In terms of basketball alone, almost everybody has to
lose. A high percentage of the convicts in Athena, and
now in this much smaller institution, devoted their
childhood and youth to nothing but basketball and still
got their brains knocked out in the early rounds of some
darn fool tournament.

Let me say further to the chance young reader that I
would probably have wrecked my body and been
thrown out of the University of Michigan and died on
Skid Row somewhere if I had not been subjected to the

discipline of West Point. I am talking about my body now, and not my mind, and there is no better way for a young person to learn respect for his or now her bones and nerves and muscles than to accept an appointment to any one of the 3 major service academies.

I entered the Point a young punk with bad posture and a sunken chest, and no history of sports participation, save for a few fights after dances where our band had played. When I graduated and received my commission as a Second Lieutenant in the Regular Army, and tossed my hat in the air, and bought a red Corvette with the back pay the Academy had put aside for me, my spine was as straight as a ramrod, my lungs were as capacious as the bellows of the forge of Vulcan, I was captain of the judo and wrestling teams, and I had not smoked any sort of cigarette or swallowed a drop of alcohol for 4 whole years! Nor was I sexually promiscuous anymore. I never felt better in my life.

I can remember saying to my mother and father at graduation, "Can this be me?"

They were so proud of me, and I was so proud of me.

I turned to Jack Patton, who was there with his booby-trapped sister and mother and his normal father, and I asked him, "What do you think of us now, Lieutenant Patton?" He was the goat of our class, meaning he had the lowest grade average. So had General George Patton been, again no relative of Jack's, who had been such a great leader in World War II.

What Jack replied, of course, unsmilingly, was that he had to laugh like hell.

7

I have been reading issues of the Tarkington College alumni magazine, *The Musketeer*, going all the way back to its first issue, which came out in 1910. It was so named in honor of Musket Mountain, a high hill not a mountain, on the western edge of the campus, at whose foot, next to the stable, so many victims of the escaped convicts are buried now.

Every proposed physical improvement of the college plant triggered a storm of protest. When Tarkington graduates came back here, they wanted it to be exactly as they remembered it. And 1 thing at least never did change, which was the size of the student body, stabilized at 300 since 1925. Meanwhile, of course, the growth of the prison population on the other side of the lake, invisible behind walls, was as irresistible as Thunder Beaver, as Niagara Falls.

Judging from letters to *The Musketeer*, I think the change that generated the most passionate resistance was the modernization of the Lutz Carillon soon after World War II, a memorial to Ernest Hubble Hiscock.

He was a Tarkington graduate who at the age of 21 was a nose-gunner on a Navy bomber whose pilot crashed his plane with a full load of bombs onto the flight deck of a Japanese aircraft carrier in the Battle of Midway during World War II.

I would have given anything to die in a war that meaningful.

Me? I was in show business, trying to get a big audience for the Government on TV by killing real people with live ammunition, something the other advertisers were not free to do.

The other advertisers had to fake everything.

Oddly enough, the actors always turned out to be a lot more believable on the little screen than we were. Real people in real trouble don't come across, somehow.

There is still so much we have to learn about TV!

Hiscock's parents, who were divorced and remarried but still friends, chipped in to have the bells mechanized, so that one person could play them by means of a keyboard. Before that, many people had to haul away on ropes, and once a bell was set swinging, it stopped swinging in its own sweet time. There was no way of damping it.

In the old days 4 of the bells were famously off-key, but beloved, and were known as "Pickle" and "Lemon" and "Big Cracked John" and "Beelzebub." The Hiscocks had them sent to Belgium, to the same bell foundry where André Lutz had been an apprentice so long ago. There they were machined and weighted to perfect pitch, their condition when I got to play them.

It can't have been music the carillon made in the old
days. Those who used to make whatever it was described it in their letters to *The Musketeer* with the same
sort of batty love and berserk gratitude I hear from
convicts when they tell me what it was like to take
heroin laced with amphetamine, and angel dust laced
with LSD, and crack alone, and on and on. I think of
all those learning-disabled kids in the old days, hauling
away on ropes with the bells clanging sweet and sour
and as loud as thunder directly overhead, and I am sure
they were finding the same undeserved happiness so
many of the convicts found in chemicals.

And haven't I myself said that the happiest parts of
my life were when I played the bells? With absolutely no
basis in reality, I felt like many an addict that I'd won,
I'd won, I'd won!

When I was made carillonneur, I taped this sign on
the door of the chamber containing the keyboard:
"Thor." That's who I felt like when I played, sending
thunderbolts down the hillside and through the industrial ruins of Scipio, and out over the lake, and up to the
walls of the prison on the other side.

There were echoes when I played—bouncing off the
empty factories and the prison walls, and arguing with
notes just leaving the bells overhead. When Lake
Mohiga was frozen, their argument was so loud that
people who had never been in the area before thought
the prison had its own set of bells, and that their carillonneur was mocking me.

And I would yell into the mad clashing of bells and
echoes, "Laugh, Jack, laugh!"

After the prison break, the College President would shoot convicts down below from the belfry. The acoustics of the valley would cause the escapees to make many wrong guesses as to where the shots were coming from.

8

In my day, the bells no longer swung. They were welded to rigid shafts. Their clappers had been removed. They were struck instead by bolts thrust by electricity from Niagara Falls. Their singing could be stopped in an instant by brakes lined with neoprene.

The room in which a dozen or more learning-disabled bell-pullers used to be zonked out of their skulls by hellishly loud cacophony contained a 3-octave keyboard against 1 wall. The holes for the ropes in the ceiling had been plugged and plastered over.

Nothing works up there anymore. The room with the keyboard and the belfry above were riddled by bullets and also bazooka shells fired by escaped convicts down below after a sniper up among the bells shot and killed 11 of them, and wounded 15 more. The sniper was the President of Tarkington College. Even though he was dead when the convicts got to him, they were so outraged that they crucified him in the loft of the stable where the students used to keep their horses, at the foot of Musket Mountain.

So a President of Tarkington, my mentor Sam Wake-field, blew his brains out with a Colt .45. And his successor, although he couldn't feel anything, was crucified.

One would have to say that that was extra-heavy history.

As for light history: The no longer useful clappers of the bells were hung in order of size, but unlabeled, on the wall of the foyer of this library, above the perpetual-motion machines. So it became a college tradition for upperclasspersons to tell incoming freshmen that the clappers were the petrified penises of different mammals. The biggest clapper, which had once belonged to Beelzebub, the biggest bell, was said to be the penis of none other than Moby Dick, the Great White Whale.

Many of the freshmen believed it, and were watched to see how long they went on believing it, just as they had been watched when they were little, no doubt, to see how long they would go on believing in the Tooth Fairy, the Easter Bunny, and Santa Claus.

Vietnam.

Most of the letters to *The Musketeer* protesting the modernization of the Lutz Carillon are from people who had somehow hung on to the wealth and power they had been born to. One, though, is from a man who admitted that he was in prison for fraud, and that he had ruined his life and that of his family with his twin addictions to alcohol and gambling. His letter was like this book, a gallows speech.

One thing he had still looked forward to, he said,

after he had paid his debt to society, was returning to
Scipio to ring the bells with ropes again.

"Now you take that away from me," he said.

One letter is from an old bell-puller, very likely dead
by now, a member of the Class of 1924 who had married
a man named Marthinus de Wet, the owner of a gold
mine in Krugersdorp, South Africa. She knew the history of the bells, that they had been made from weapons
gathered up after the Battle of Gettysburg. She did not
mind that the bells would soon be played electrically.
The bad idea, as far as she was concerned, was that the
sour bells, Pickle and Lemon and Big Cracked John and
Beelzebub, were going to be turned on lathes in Belgium
until they were either in tune or on the scrap heap.

"Are Tarkington students no longer to be humanized
and humbled as I was day after day," she asked, "by the
cries from the bell tower of the dying on the sacred,
blood-soaked grounds of Gettysburg?"

The bells controversy inspired a lot of purple prose
like that, much of it dictated to a secretary or a machine,
no doubt. It is quite possible that Mrs. de Wet graduated from Tarkington without being able to write any
better than most of the ill-educated prisoners across the
lake.

If my Socialist grandfather, nothing but a gardener at
Butler University, could read the letter from Mrs. de
Wet and note its South African return address, he
would be grimly gratified. There was a clear-as-crystal
demonstration of a woman living high on profits from
the labor of black miners, overworked and underpaid.

He would have seen exploitation of the poor and
powerless in the growth of the prison across the lake as

well. The prison to him would have been a scheme for depriving the lower social orders of leadership in the Class Struggle and for providing them with a horrible alternative to accepting whatever their greedy paymasters would give them in the way of working conditions and subsistence.

By the time I got to Tarkington College, though, he would have been wrong about the meaning of the prison across the lake, since poor and powerless people, no matter how docile, were no longer of use to canny investors. What they used to do was now being done by heroic and uncomplaining machinery.

So an appropriate sign to put over the gate to Athena might have been, instead of "Work Makes Free," for example: "Too bad you were born. Nobody has any use for you," or maybe: "Come in and stay in, all you burdens on Society."

9

A former roommate of Ernest Hubble Hiscock, the dead war hero, who had also been in the war, who had lost an arm as a Marine on Iwo Jima, wrote that the memorial Hiscock himself would have wanted most was a promise by the Board of Trustees at the start of each academic year to keep the enrollment the same size it had been in his time.

So if Ernest Hubble Hiscock is looking down from Heaven now, or wherever it is that war heroes go after dying, he would be dismayed to see his beloved campus surrounded by barbed wire and watchtowers. The bells are shot to hell. The number of students, if you can call convicts that, is about 2,000 now.

When there were only 300 "students" here, each one had a bedroom and a bathroom and plenty of closets all his or her own. Each bedroom was part of a 2-bedroom, 2-bathroom suite with a common living room for 2. Each living room had couches and easy chairs and a working fireplace, and state-of-the-art sound-reproduction equipment and a big-screen TV.

At the Athena state prison, as I would discover when I went to work over there, there were 6 men to each cell and each cell had been built for 2. Each 50 cells had a recreation room with one Ping-Pong table and one TV. The TV, moreover, showed only tapes of programs, including news, at least 10 years old. The idea was to keep the prisoners from becoming distressed about anything going on in the outside world that hadn't been all taken care of one way or the other, presumably, in the long-ago.

They could feast their eyes on whatever they liked, just so long as it wasn't relevant.

How those letter-writers loved not just the college but the whole Mohiga Valley—the seasons, the lake, the forest primeval on the other side. And there were few differences between student pleasures in their times and my own. In my time, students didn't skate on the lake anymore, but on an indoor rink given in 1971 by the Israel Cohen Family. But they still had sailboat races and canoe races on the lake. They still had picnics by the ruins of the locks at the head of the lake. Many students still brought their own horses to school with them. In my time, several students brought not just 1 horse but 3, since polo was a major sport. In 1976 and again in 1980, Tarkington College had an undefeated polo team.

There are no horses in the stable now, of course. The escaped convicts, surrounded and starving a mere 4 days after the prison break, calling themselves "Freedom Fighters" and flying an American flag from the top of the bell tower of this library, ate the horses and the campus dogs, too, and fed pieces of them to their hostages, who were the Trustees of the college.

The most successful athlete ever to come from Tarkington, arguably, was a horseman from my own time, Lowell Chung. He won a Bronze Medal as a member of the United States Equestrian Team in Seoul, South Korea, back in 1988. His mother owned half of Honolulu, but he couldn't read or write or do math worth a darn. He could sure do Physics, though. He could tell me how levers and lenses and electricity and heat and all sorts of power plants worked, and predict correctly what an experiment would prove before I'd performed it—just as long as I didn't insist that he quantify anything, that he tell me what the numbers were.

He earned his Associate in the Arts and Sciences Degree in 1984. That was the only degree we awarded, fair warning to other institutions and future employers, and to the students themselves, that our graduates' intellectual achievements, while respectable, were unconventional.

Lowell Chung got me on a horse for the first time in my life when I was 43 years old. He dared me. I told him I certainly wasn't going to commit suicide on the back of one of his firecracker polo ponies, since I had a wife and a mother-in-law and 2 children to support. So he borrowed a gentle, patient old mare from his girlfriend at the time, who was Claudia Roosevelt.

Comically enough, Lowell's then girlfriend was a whiz at arithmetic, but otherwise a nitwit. You could ask her, "What is 5,111 times 10,022, divided by 97?"

Claudia would reply, "That's 528,066.4. So what? So what?"

So what indeed! The lesson I myself learned over and over again when teaching at the college and then the prison was the uselessness of information to most people, except as entertainment. If facts weren't funny or scary, or couldn't make you rich, the heck with them.

When I later went to work at the prison, I encountered a mass murderer named Alton Darwin who also could do arithmetic in his head. He was Black. Unlike Claudia Roosevelt, he was highly intelligent in the verbal area. The people he had murdered were rivals or deadbeats or police informers or cases of mistaken identity or innocent bystanders in the illegal drug industry. His manner of speaking was elegant and thought-provoking.

He hadn't killed nearly as many people as I had. But then again, he hadn't had my advantage, which was the full cooperation of our Government.

Also, he had done all his killing for reasons of money. I had never stooped to that.

When I found out that he could do arithmetic in his head, I said to him, "That's a remarkable gift you have."

"Doesn't seem fair, does it," he said, "that somebody should come into the world with such a great advantage over the common folk? When I get out of here, I'm going to buy me a pretty striped tent and put up a sign saying 'One dollar. Come on in and see the Nigger do arithmetic.' " He wasn't ever going to get out of there. He was serving a life sentence without hope of parole.

Darwin's fantasy about starring in a mental-arithmetic show when he got out, incidentally, was inspired by something 1 of his great-grandfathers did in South Carolina after World War I. All the airplane pilots back then were white, and some of them did stunt flying at country fairs. They were called "barnstormers."

And 1 of these barnstormers with a 2-cockpit plane strapped Darwin's great-grandfather in the front cockpit, even though the great-grandfather couldn't even drive an automobile. The barnstormer crouched down in the rear cockpit, so people couldn't see him but he could still work the controls. And people came from far and wide, according to Darwin, "to see the Nigger fly the airplane."

He was only 25 years old when we first met, the same age as Lowell Chung when Lowell won the Bronze Medal for horseback riding in Seoul, South Korea. When I was 25, I hadn't killed anybody yet, and hadn't had nearly as many women as Darwin had. When he was only 20, he told me, he paid cash for a Ferrari. I didn't have a car of my own, which was a good car, all right, a Chevrolet Corvette, but nowhere near as good as a Ferrari, until I was 21.

At least I, too, had paid cash.

When we talked at the prison, he had a running joke that was the assumption that we came from different planets. The prison was all there was to his planet, and I had come in a flying saucer from one that was much bigger and wiser.

This enabled him to comment ironically on the only sexual activities possible inside the walls. "You have little babies on your planet?" he asked.

"Yes, we have little babies," I said.

"We got people here trying to have babies every which way," he said, "but they never get babies. What do you think they're doing wrong?"

He was the first convict I heard use the expression "the PB." He told me that sometimes he wished he had "the PB." I thought he meant "TB," short for "tuberculosis," another common affliction at the prison—common enough that I have it now.

It turned out that "PB" was short for "Parole Board," which is what the convicts called AIDS.

That was when we first met, back in 1991, when he said that sometimes he wished he had the PB, and long before I myself contracted TB.

Alphabet soup!

He was hungry for descriptions of this valley, to which he had been sentenced for the rest of his life and where he could expect to be buried, but which he had never seen. Not only the convicts but their visitors, too, were kept as ignorant as possible of the precise geographical situation of the prison, so that anybody escaping would have no clear idea of what to watch out for or which way to go.

Visitors were brought into the cul-de-sac of the valley from Rochester in buses with blacked-out windows. Convicts themselves were delivered in windowless steel boxes capable of holding 10 of them wearing leg irons and handcuffs, mounted on the beds of trucks. The buses and the steel boxes were never opened until they were well inside the prison walls.

These were exceedingly dangerous and resourceful criminals, after all. While the Japanese had taken over the operation of Athena by the time I got there, hoping to operate it at a profit, the blacked-out buses and steel boxes had been in use long before they got there. Those morbid forms of transportation became a common sight on the road to and from Rochester in maybe 1977, about 2 years after I and my little family took up residence in Scipio.

The only change the Japanese made in the vehicles, which was under way when I went to work over there in 1991, was to remount the old steel boxes on new Japanese trucks.

So it was in violation of long-standing prison policy that I told Alton Darwin and other lifers all they wanted to know about the valley. I thought they were entitled to know about the great forest, which was their forest now, and the beautiful lake, which was their lake now, and the beautiful little college, which was where the music from the bells was coming from.

And of course, this enriched their dreams of escaping, but what were those but what we could call in any other context the virtue hope? I never thought they would ever really get out of here and make use of the knowledge I had given them of the countryside, and neither did they.

I used to do the same sort of thing in Vietnam, too, helping mortally wounded soldiers dream that they would soon be well and home again.

Why not?

I am as sorry as anybody that Darwin and all the rest really tasted freedom. They were horrible news for themselves and everyone. A lot of them were real homicidal maniacs. Darwin wasn't 1 of those, but even as the convicts were crossing the ice to Scipio, he was giving orders as if he were an Emperor, as if the break were his idea, although he had had nothing to do with it. He hadn't known it was coming.

Those who had actually breached the walls and opened the cells had come down from Rochester to free only 1 convict. They got him, and they were headed out of the valley and had no interest in conquering Scipio and its little army of 6 regular policemen and 3 unarmed campus cops, and an unknown number of firearms in private hands.

Alton Darwin was the first example I had ever seen of leadership in the raw. He was a man without any badges of rank, and with no previously existing organization or widely understood plan of action. He had been a modest, unremarkable man in prison. The moment he got out, though, sudden delusions of grandeur made him the only man who knew what to do next, which was to attack Scipio, where glory and riches awaited all who dared to follow him.

"Follow me!" he cried, and some did. He was a sociopath, I think, in love with himself and no one else, craving action for its own sake, and indifferent to any long-term consequences, a classic Man of Destiny.

Most did not even follow him down the slope and out onto the ice. They returned to the prison, where they had beds of their own, and shelter from the weather, and food and water, although no heat or electricity. They chose to be good boys, concluding correctly that bad boys roaming free in the valley, but completely surrounded by the forces of law and order, would be shot on sight in a day or 2, or maybe even sooner. They were color-coded, after all.

In the Mohiga Valley, their skin alone sufficed as a prison uniform.

About half of those who followed Darwin out onto the ice turned back before they reached Scipio. This was before they were fired upon and suffered their first casualty. One of those who went back to the prison told me that he was sickened when he realized how much murder and rape there would be when they reached the other side in just a few minutes.

"I thought about all the little children fast asleep in their beds," he said. He had handed over the gun he had stolen from the prison armory to the man next to him, there in the middle of beautiful Lake Mohiga. "He didn't have a gun," he said, "until I gave him 1."

"Did you wish each other good luck or anything like that?" I asked him.

"We didn't say anything," he told me. "Nobody was saying anything but the man in front."

"And what was he saying?" I asked.

He replied with terrible emptiness, " 'Follow me, follow me, follow me.' "

"Life's a bad dream," he said. "Do you know that?"

Alton Darwin's charismatic delusions of grandeur went on and on. He declared himself to be President of a new country. He set up his headquarters in the Board of Trustees Room of Samoza Hall, with the big long table for his desk.

I visited him there at high noon on the second day after the great escape. He told me that this new country of his was going to cut down the virgin forest on the other side of the lake and sell the wood to the Japanese. He would use the money to refurbish the abandoned industrial buildings in Scipio down below. He didn't know yet what they would manufacture, but he was thinking hard about that. He would welcome any suggestions I might have.

Nobody would dare attack him, he said, for fear he would harm his hostages. He held the entire Board of Trustees captive, but not the College President, Henry "Tex" Johnson, nor his wife, Zuzu. I had come to ask Darwin if he had any idea what had become of Tex and Zuzu. He didn't know.

Zuzu, it would turn out, had been killed by a person or persons unknown, possibly raped, possibly not. We will never know. It was not an ideal time for Forensic Medicine. Tex, meanwhile, was ascending the tower of the library here with a rifle and ammunition. He was going clear to the top, to turn the belfry itself into a sniper's nest.

Alton Darwin was never worried, no matter how bad things got. He laughed when he heard that paratroops, advancing on foot, had surrounded the prison across the lake and, on our side, were digging in to the west and south of Scipio. State Police and vigilantes had already set up a roadblock at the head of the lake. Alton Darwin laughed as though he had achieved a great victory.

I knew people like that in Vietnam. Jack Patton had that sort of courage. I could be as brave as Jack over there. In fact, I am pretty sure that I was shot at more and killed more people. But I was worried sick most of the time. Jack never worried. He told me so.

I asked him how he could be that way. He said, "I think I must have a screw loose. I can't care about what might happen next to me or anyone."

Alton Darwin had the same untightened screw. He was a convicted mass murderer, but never showed any remorse that I could see.

During my last year in Vietnam, I, too, reacted at press briefings as though our defeats were victories. But I was under orders to do that. That wasn't my natural disposition.

Alton Darwin, and this was true of Jack Patton, too, spoke of trivial and serious matters in the same tone of voice, with the same gestures and facial expressions. Nothing mattered more or less than anything else.

Alton Darwin, I remember, was talking to me with seemingly deep concern about how many of the convicts who had crossed the ice with him to Scipio were deserting, were going back across the ice to the prison, or turning themselves in at the roadblock at the head of the lake in hopes of amnesty. The deserters were worriers. They didn't want to die, and they didn't want to be held responsible, even though many of them were responsible, for the murders and rapes in Scipio.

So I was pondering the desertion problem when Alton Darwin said with exactly the same intensity, "I can skate on ice. Do you believe that?"

"I beg your pardon?" I said.

"I could always roller-skate," he said. "But I never got a chance to ice-skate till this morning."

That morning, with the phones dead and the electricity cut off, with unburied bodies everywhere, and with all the food in Scipio already consumed as though by a locust plague, he had gone up to Cohen Rink and put on ice skates for the first time in his life. After a few tottering steps, he had found himself gliding around and around, and around and around.

"Roller-skating and ice-skating are just about the very same thing!" he told me triumphantly, as though he had made a scientific discovery that was going to throw an entirely new light on what had seemed a hopeless situation. "Same muscles!" he said importantly.

That's what he was doing when he was fatally shot about an hour later. He was out on the rink, gliding around and around, and around and around. I'd left him in his office, and I assumed that he was still up there. But there he was on the rink instead, going around and around, and around and around.

A shot rang out, and he fell down.

Several of his followers went to him, and he said something to them, and then he died.

It was a beautiful shot, if Darwin was really the man the College President was shooting at. He could have been shooting at me, since he knew I used to make love to his wife Zuzu when he was out of the house.

If he was shooting at Darwin instead of me, he solved one of the most difficult problems in marksmanship, the same problem solved by Lee Harvey Oswald when he shot President Kennedy, which is where to aim when you are high above your target.

As I say, "Beautiful shot."

I asked later what Alton Darwin's last words had been, and was told that they made no sense. His last words had been, "See the Nigger fly the airplane."

10

Sometimes Alton Darwin would talk to me about the planet he was on before he was transported in a steel box to Athena. "Drugs were food," he said. "I was in the food business. Just because people on one planet eat a certain kind of food they're hungry for, that makes them feel better after they eat it, that doesn't mean people on other planets shouldn't eat something else. On some planets I'm sure there are people who eat stones, and then feel wonderful for a little while afterwards. Then it's time to eat stones again."

I thought very little about the prison during the 15 years I was a teacher at Tarkington, as big and brutal as it was across the lake, and growing all the time. When we went picnicking at the head of the lake, or went up to Rochester on some errand or other, I saw plenty of blacked-out buses and steel boxes on the backs of trucks. Alton Darwin might have been in one of those boxes. Then again, since the steel boxes were also used to carry freight, there might have been nothing but Diet Pepsi and toilet paper in there.

Whatever was in there was none of my business until Tarkington fired me.

Sometimes when I was playing the bells and getting particularly loud echoes from the prison walls, usually in the dead of the wintertime, I would have the feeling that I was shelling the prison. In Vietnam, conversely, if I happened to be back with the artillery, and the guns were lobbing shells at who knows what in some jungle, it seemed very much like music, interesting noises for the sake of interesting noises, and nothing more.

During a summer field exercise when Jack Patton and I were still cadets, I remember, we were asleep in a tent and the artillery opened up nearby.

We awoke. Jack said to me, "They're playing our tune, Gene. They're playing our tune."

Before I went to work at Athena, I had seen only 3 convicts anywhere in the valley. Most people in Scipio hadn't seen even 1. I wouldn't have seen even 1, either, if a truck with a steel box in back hadn't broken down at the head of the lake. I was picnicking there, near the water, with Margaret, my wife, and Mildred, my mother-in-law. Mildred was crazy as a bedbug by then, but Margaret was still sane, and there seemed a good chance that she always would be.

I was only 45, foolishly confident that I would go on teaching here until I reached the mandatory retirement age of 70 in 2010, 9 years from now. What in fact will happen to me in 9 more years? That is like worrying about a cheese spoiling if you don't put it in the refriger-

ator. What can happen to a pricelessly stinky cheese
that hasn't already happened to it?

My mother-in-law, no danger to herself or anyone
else, adored fishing. I had put a worm on her hook for
her and pitched it out to a spot that looked promising.
She gripped the rod with both hands, sure as always
that something miraculous was about to happen.

She was right this time.

I looked up at the top of the bank, and there was a
prison truck with smoke pouring out of its engine com-
partment. There were only 2 guards on board, and 1 of
them was the driver. They bailed out. They had already
radioed the prison for help. They were both white. This
was before the Japanese took over Athena as a business
proposition, before the road signs all the way from
Rochester were in both English and Japanese.

It looked as though the truck might catch fire, so the
2 guards unlocked the little door in the back of the steel
box and told the prisoners to come out. And then they
backed off and waited with sawed-off automatic shot-
guns leveled at the little door.

Out the prisoners came. There were only 3 of them,
clumsy in leg irons, and their handcuffs were shackled to
chains around their waists. Two were black and 1 was
white, or possibly a light Hispanic. This was before the
Supreme Court confirmed that it was indeed cruel and
inhuman punishment to confine a person in a place
where his or her race was greatly outnumbered by another 1.

The races were still mixed in prisons throughout the
country. When I later went to work at Athena, though,
there was nothing but people who had been classified as
Black in there.

My mother-in-law did not turn around to see the smoking van and all. She was obsessed by what might happen at any moment at the other end of her fishline. But Margaret and I gawked. For us back then, prisoners were like pornography, common things nice people shouldn't want to see, even though the biggest industry by far in this valley was punishment.

When Margaret and I talked about it later, she didn't say it was like pornography. She said it was like seeing animals on their way to a slaughterhouse.

We, in turn, must have looked to those convicts like people in Paradise. It was a balmy day in the springtime. A sailboat race was going on to the south of us. The college had just been given 30 little sloops by a grateful parent who had cleaned out the biggest savings and loan bank in California.

Our brand-new Mercedes sedan was parked on the beach nearby. It cost more than my annual salary at Tarkington. The car was a gift from the mother of a student of mine named Pierre LeGrand. His maternal grandfather had been dictator of Haiti, and had taken the treasury of that country with him when he was overthrown. That was why Pierre's mother was so rich. He was very unpopular. He tried to win friends by making expensive gifts to them, but that didn't work, so he tried to hang himself from a girder of the water tower on top of Musket Mountain. I happened to be up there, in the bushes with the wife of the coach of the Tennis Team.

So I cut him down with my Swiss Army knife. That was how I got the Mercedes.

Pierre would have better luck 2 years later, jumping

off the Golden Gate Bridge, and a campus joke was that now I had to give the Mercedes back.

So there were plenty of heartaches in what, as I've said, must have looked to those 3 convicts like Paradise. There was no way they could tell that my mother-in-law was as crazy as a bedbug, as long as she kept her back to them. They could not know, and neither could I, of course, that hereditary insanity would hit my pretty wife like a ton of bricks in about 6 months' time and turn her into a hag as scary as her mother.

If we had had our 2 kids with us on the beach, that would have completed the illusion that we lived in Paradise. They could have depicted another generation that found life as comfortable as we did. Both sexes would have been represented. We had a girl named Melanie and a boy named Eugene Debs Hartke, Jr. But they weren't kids anymore. Melanie was 21, and studying mathematics at Cambridge University in England. Eugene Jr. was completing his senior year at Deerfield Academy in Massachusetts, and was 18, and had his own rock-and-roll band, and had composed maybe 100 songs by then.

But Melanie would have spoiled our tableau on the beach. Like my mother until she went to Weight Watchers, she was very heavy. That must be hereditary. If she had kept her back to the convicts, she might at least have concealed the fact that she had a bulbous nose like the late, great, alcoholic comedian W.C. Fields. Melanie, thank goodness, was not also an alcoholic.

But her brother was.

And I could kill myself now for having boasted to him that on my side of the family the men had no fear of alcohol, since they knew how to drink in moderation.

We were not weak and foolish where drugs were concerned.

At least Eugene Jr. was beautiful, having inherited the features of his mother. When he was growing up in this valley, people could not resist saying to me, with him right there to hear it, that he was the most beautiful child they'd ever seen.

I have no idea where he is now. He stopped communicating with me or anybody in this valley years ago.

He hates me.

So does Melanie, although she wrote to me as recently as 2 years ago. She was living in Paris with another woman. They were both teaching English and math in an American high school over there.

My kids will never forgive me for not putting my mother-in-law into a mental hospital instead of keeping her at home, where she was a great embarrassment to them. They couldn't bring friends home. If I had put Mildred into a nuthouse, though, I couldn't have afforded to send Melanie and Eugene Jr. to such expensive schools. I got a free house at Tarkington, but my salary was small.

Also, I didn't think Mildred's craziness was as unbearable as they did. In the Army I had grown used to people who talked nonsense all day long. Vietnam was 1 big hallucination. After adjusting to that, I could adjust to anything.

What my children most dislike me for, though, is my reproducing in conjunction with their mother. They live in constant dread of suddenly going as batty as Mildred and Margaret. Unfortunately, there is a good chance of that.

Ironically enough, I happen to have an illegitimate son about whom I learned only recently. Since he had a different mother, he need not expect to go insane someday. Some of his kids, if he ever has any, could inherit my own mother's tendency to fatness, though.

But they could join Weight Watchers as Mother did.

Heredity is obviously much on my mind these days, and should be. So I have been reading up on it some in a book that also deals with embryology. And I tell you: People who are wary of what they might find in a book if they opened 1 are right to be. I have just had my mind blown by an essay on the embryology of the human eye.

No combination of Time and Luck could have produced a camera that excellent, not even if the quantity of time had been 1,000,000,000,000 years! How is that for an unsolved mystery?

When I went to work at Athena, I hoped to find at least 1 of the 3 convicts who had seen Mildred and Margaret and me having a picnic so long ago. As I've said, I took 1 of them to be a White, or possibly Hispanic. So he would have been transferred to a White or Hispanic prison before I ever got there. The other 2 were clearly black, but I never found either of them. I would have liked to hear what we looked like to them, how contented we seemed to be.

They were probably dead. AIDS could have got them, or murder or suicide, or maybe tuberculosis. Every year, 30 inmates at Athena died for every student who was awarded an Associate in the Arts and Sciences Degree by Tarkington.

Parole.

If I had found a convict who had witnessed our picnic, we might have talked about the fish my mother-in-law hooked while he was watching. He saw her rod bend double, heard the reel scream like a little siren. But he never got to see the monster who had taken her bait and was headed south for Scipio. Before he could see it, he was back in darkness in another van.

It was heavy test line I had put on the reel. This was deep-sea stuff made for tuna and shark, although, as far as we knew, there was nothing in Lake Mohiga but eels and perch and little catfish. That was all Mildred had ever caught before.

One time, I remember, she caught a perch too little to keep. So I turned it loose, even though the barb of the hook had come out through one eye. A few minutes later she hooked that same perch again. We could tell by the mangled eye. Think about that. Miraculous eyes, and no brains whatsoever.

I put such heavy test line on Mildred's reel so that nothing could ever get away from her. In Honduras 1 time I did the same thing for a 3-star General, whose aide I was.

Mildred's fish couldn't snap the line, and Mildred wouldn't let go of the rod. She didn't weigh anything, and the fish weighed a lot for a fish. Mildred went down on her knees in the water, laughing and crying.

I'll never forget what she was saying: "It's God! It's God!"

I waded out to help her. She wouldn't let go of the rod, so I grasped the line and began to haul it in, hand over hand.

How the water swirled and boiled out there!

When I got the fish into shallow water, it suddenly quit fighting. I guess it had used up every bit of its energy. That was that.

This fish, which I picked up by the gills and flung up on the bank, was an enormous pickerel. Margaret looked down at it in horror and said, "It's a crocodile!"

I looked at the top of the bank to see what the convicts and guards thought of a fish that big. They were gone. There was nothing but the broken-down van up there. The little door to its steel box was wide open. Anybody was free to climb inside and close the door, in case he or she wondered what it felt like to be a prisoner.

To those fascinated by Forensic Medicine: The pickerel had not bitten on the worm on the hook. It had bitten on a perch which had bitten on the worm on the hook.

I thought that would be interesting to my mother-in-law during our trip back home in the new Mercedes. But she didn't want to talk about the fish at all. It had scared the daylights out of her, and she wanted to forget it.

As the years went by, I would mention the fish from time to time without getting anything back from her but a stony silence. I concluded that she really had purged it from her memory.

But then, on the night of the prison break, when the 3 of us were living in an old house in the hamlet of

Athena, down below the prison walls, there was this terrific explosion that woke us up.

If Jack Patton had been there with us, he might have said to me, "Gene! Gene! They're playing our tune again."

The explosion was in fact the demolition of Athena's main gate from the outside, not the inside. The purported head of the Jamaican drug cartel, Jeffrey Turner, had been brought down to Athena in a steel box 6 months before, after a televised trial lasting a year and a half. He was given 25 consecutive life sentences, said to be a new record. Now a well-rehearsed force of his employees, variously estimated as being anything from a platoon to a company, had arrived outside the prison with explosives, a tank, and several half-tracks taken from the National Guard Armory about 10 kilometers south of Rochester, across the highway from the Meadowdale Cinema Complex. One of their number, it has since come out, moved to Rochester and joined the National Guard, swearing to defend the Constitution and all that, with the sole purpose of stealing the keys to the Armory.

The Japanese guards were wholly unprepared and unmotivated to resist such a force, especially since the attackers were all dressed in American Army uniforms and waving American flags. So they hid or put their hands up or ran off into the virgin forest. This wasn't their country, and guarding prisoners wasn't a sacred mission or anything like that. It was just a business.

The telephone and power lines were cut, so they couldn't even call for help or blow the siren.

The assault lasted half an hour. When it was over, Jeffrey Turner was gone, and he hasn't been seen since. The attackers also disappeared. Their uniforms and

military vehicles were subsequently found at an abandoned dairy farm owned by German land speculators a
kilometer north of the end of the lake. There were tire
tracks of many automobiles, which led police to conclude that it was by means of unremarkable civilian
vehicles, seemingly unrelated, and no doubt leaving the
farm at timed intervals, that the lawless force had made
its 100-percent-successful getaway.

Meanwhile, back at the prison, anyone who didn't
want to stay inside the walls anymore was free to walk
out of there, first taking, if he was so inclined and got
there early, a rifle or a shotgun or a pistol or a tear-gas
grenade from the wide-open prison armory.

The police said, too, that the attackers of the prison
obviously had had first-class military training somewhere, possibly at a private survival school somewhere
in this country, or maybe in Bolivia or Colombia or
Peru.

Anyway: Margaret and Mildred and I were awak-
ened by the explosion, which demolished the main gate
of the prison. There was no way we could have imagined what was really going on.

The 3 of us were sleeping in separate bedrooms. Margaret was on the first floor, Mildred and I were on the
second floor. No sooner had I sat up, my ears ringing,
than Mildred came into my room stark naked, her eyes
open wide.

She spoke first. She used a slang word for hugeness I
had never heard her speak before. It wasn't slang of her
generation or even mine. It was slang of my children's
generation. I guess she had heard it and liked it, and

then held it in reserve for some really important occasion.

Here is what she said, as sporadic small-arms fire broke out at the prison: "Do you remember that *humongous* fish I caught?"

11

At one time I fully expected to spend the rest of my life in this valley, but not in jail. I envisioned my mandatory retirement from Tarkington College in 2010. I would be modestly well-off with Social Security and a pension from the College. My mother-in-law would surely be dead by then, I thought, so I would have only Margaret to care for. I would rent a little house in the town below. There were plenty of empty ones.

But that dream would have been blasted even if there hadn't been a prison break, even if the Social Security system hadn't gone bust and the College Treasurer hadn't run off with the pension funds and so on. For, as I've said before, in 1991 Tarkington College fired me.

There I was in late middle age, cut loose in a thoroughly looted, bankrupt nation whose assets had been sold off to foreigners, a nation swamped by unchecked plagues and superstition and illiteracy and hypnotic TV, with virtually no health services for the poor. Where to go? What to do?

The man who got me fired was Jason Wilder, the celebrated Conservative newspaper columnist, lecturer, and television talk-show host. He saved my life by doing that. If it weren't for him, I would have been on the Scipio side of the lake instead of the Athena side during the prison break.

I would have been facing all those convicts as they crossed the ice to Scipio in the moonlight, instead of watching them in mute wonderment from the rear, like Robert E. Lee during Pickett's Charge at the Battle of Gettysburg. They wouldn't have known me, and I would still have seen only 3 Athena convicts in all my time.

I would have tried to fight in some way, although, unlike the College President, I would have had no guns. I would have been killed and buried along with the College President and his wife Zuzu, and Alton Darwin and all the rest of them. I would have been buried next to the stable, in the shadow of Musket Mountain when the Sun went down.

The first time I saw Jason Wilder in person was at the Board meeting when they fired me. He was then only an outraged parent. He would later join the Board and become by far the most valuable of the convicts' hostages after the prison break. Their threat to kill him immobilized units of the 82nd Airborne Division, which had been brought in by school bus from the South Bronx. The paratroops sealed off the valley at the head of the lake and occupied the shoreline across from Scipio and to the south of Scipio, and dug in on the western slope of Musket Mountain. But they dared not come any closer, for fear of causing the death of Jason Wilder.

There were other hostages, to be sure, including the rest of the Trustees, but he was the only famous one. I myself was not strictly a hostage, although I would probably have been killed if I had tried to leave. I was a sort of floating, noncombatant wise man, wandering wherever I pleased in Scipio under siege. As at Athena Prison, I tried to give the most honest answer I could to any question anyone might care to put to me. Otherwise I stayed silent. I volunteered no advice at Athena, and none in Scipio under siege. I simply described the truth of the inquirer's situation in the context of the world outside as best I could. What he did next was up to him.

I call that being a teacher. I don't call that being a mastermind of a treasonous enterprise. All I ever wanted to overthrow was ignorance and self-serving fantasies.

I was fired without warning on Graduation Day. I was playing the bells at high noon when a girl who had just completed her freshman year brought the news that the Board of Trustees, then meeting in Samoza Hall, the administration building, wanted to talk to me. She was Kimberley Wilder, Jason Wilder's learning-disabled daughter. She was stupid. I thought it was odd but not menacing that the Trustees would have used her for a messenger. I couldn't imagine what business she might have had that would bring her anywhere near their meeting. She had in fact been testifying before them about my supposed lack of patriotism, and had then asked for the honor of fetching me to my liquidation.

She was one of the few underclasspersons still on the campus. The rest had gone home, and relatives of those

about to get their Associate in the Arts and Sciences
certificates had taken over their suites. No relative of
Kimberley's was about to graduate. She had stayed
around for the Trustees' meeting. And her famous father had come by helicopter to back her up. The soccer
field was being used as a heliport. It looked like a rook-
ery for pterodactyls.

Others had arrived in conventional aircraft at
Rochester, where they had been met by rented limou-
sines provided by the college. One senior's stepmother
said, I remember, that she thought she had landed in
Yokohama instead of Rochester because there were so
many Japanese. The thing was that the changing of the
guard at Athena had coincided with Graduation Day.
New guards, mostly country boys from Hokkaido, who
spoke no English and had never seen the United States,
were flown directly to Rochester from Tokyo every 6
months, and taken to Athena by bus. And then those
who had served 6 months at the gates, and on the walls
and catwalks over the mess halls, and in the watchtowers, and so on, were flown straight home.

"How come you haven't gone home, Kimberley?" I
said.

She said that she and her father wanted to hear the
graduation address, which was to be delivered by her
father's close friend and fellow Rhodes Scholar, Dr.
Martin Peale Blankenship, the University of Chicago
economist who would later become a quadriplegic as a
result of a skiing accident in Switzerland.

Dr. Blankenship had a niece in the graduating class.
That was what brought him to Scipio. His niece was
Hortense Mellon. I have no idea what became of Hor-
tense. She could play the harp. I remember that, and her

upper teeth were false. The real teeth were knocked out
by a mugger as she left a friend's coming-out party at
the Waldorf-Astoria, which has since burned down.
There is nothing but a vacant lot there now, which was
bought by the Japanese.

I heard that her father, like so many other Tarkington parents, lost an awful lot of money in the biggest
swindle in the history of Wall Street, stock in a company
called Microsecond Arbitrage.

I had spotted Kimberley as a snoop, all right, but not
as a walking recording studio. All through the academic
year now ending, our paths had crossed with puzzling
frequency. Again and again I would be talking to somebody, almost anywhere on the campus, and realize that
Kimberley was lurking close by. I assumed that she was
slightly cracked, and was eavesdropping on everyone,
avid for gossip. She wasn't even taking a course of mine
for credit, although she did audit both Physics for Non-
scientists and Music Appreciation for Nonmusicians.
So what could I possibly be to her or she to me? We had
never had a conversation about anything.

One time, I remember, I was shooting pool in the new
recreation center, the Pahlavi Pavilion, and she was so
close that I was having trouble working my cuestick,
and I said to her, "Do you like my perfume?"

"What?" she said.

"I find you so close to me so often," I said, "I thought
maybe you liked my perfume. I'm very flattered, if
that's the case, because that's nothing but my natural
body odor. I don't use perfume."

I can quote myself exactly, since those words were on
one of the tapes the Trustees would play back for me.
She shrugged as though she didn't know what I was

talking about. She didn't leave the Pavilion in great embarrassment. On the contrary! She gave me a little more room for my cuestick but was still practically on top of me.

I was playing 8-ball head to head with the novelist Paul Slazinger, that year's Writer in Residence. He was dead broke and out of print, which is the only reason anybody ever became Writer in Residence at Tarkington. He was so old that he had actually been in World War II. He had won a Silver Star like me when I was only 3 years old!

He asked me who Kimberley was, and I said, and she got this on tape, too, "Pay no attention. She's just another member of the Ruling Class."

So the Board of Trustees would want to know what it was, exactly, that I had against the Ruling Class.

I didn't say so back then, but I am perfectly happy to say now that the trouble with the Ruling Class was that too many of its members were nitwits like Kimberley.

One theory I had about her snooping was that she was titillated by my reputation as the campus John F. Kennedy as far as sex outside of marriage was concerned.

If President Kennedy up in Heaven ever made a list of all the women he had made love to, I am sure it would be 2 or 3 times as long as the one I am making down here in jail. Then again, he had the glamour of his office, and the full cooperation of the Secret Service and the White House Staff. None of the names on my list would mean anything to the general public, whereas many on his would belong to movie stars. He made love to Marilyn Monroe. I sure never did. She evidently expected to marry him and become First Lady, which was a joke to everybody but her.

She eventually committed suicide. She finally found life too embarrassing.

I still hardly knew Kimberley when she appeared in the bell tower on Graduation Day. But she was chatty, as though we were old, old pals. She was still recording me, although what she already had on tape was enough to do me in.

She asked me if I thought the speech Paul Slazinger, the Writer in Residence, gave in Chapel had been a good one. This was probably the most anti-American speech I had ever heard. He gave it right before Christmas vacation, and was never again seen in Scipio. He had just won a so-called Genius Grant from the MacArthur Foundation, $50,000 a year for 5 years. On the same night of his speech he bugged out for Key West, Florida.

He predicted, I remember, that human slavery would come back, that it had in fact never gone away. He said that so many people wanted to come here because it was so easy to rob the poor people, who got absolutely no protection from the Government. He talked about bridges falling down and water mains breaking because of no maintenance. He talked about oil spills and radioactive waste and poisoned aquifers and looted banks and liquidated corporations. "And nobody ever gets punished for anything," he said. "Being an American means never having to say you're sorry."

On and on he went. No matter what he said, he was still going to get $50,000 a year for 5 years.

I said to Kimberley that I thought Slazinger had said some things which were worth considering, but that, on the whole, he had made the country sound a lot worse than it really was, and that ours was still far and away the best one on the planet.

She could not have gotten much satisfaction from that reply.

What do I myself make of that reply nowadays? It was an inane reply.

She asked me about my own lecture in Chapel only a month earlier. She hadn't attended and so hadn't taped it. She was seeking confirmation of things other people had said I said. My lecture had been humorous recollections of my maternal grandfather, Benjamin Wills, the old-time Socialist.

She accused me of saying that all rich people were drunks and lunatics. This was a garbling of Grandfather's saying that Capitalism was what the people with all our money, drunk or sober, sane or insane, decided to do today. So I straightened that out, and explained that the opinion was my grandfather's, not my own.

"I heard your speech was worse than Mr. Slazinger's," she said.

"I certainly hope not," I said. "I was trying to show how outdated my grandfather's opinions were. I wanted people to laugh. They did."

"I heard you said Jesus Christ was un-American," she said, her tape recorder running all the time.

So I unscrambled that one for her. The original had been another of Grandfather's sayings. He repeated Karl Marx's prescription for an ideal society, "From each according to his abilities, to each according to his needs." And then he asked me, meaning it to be a wry

joke, "What could be more un-American, Gene, than
sounding like the Sermon on the Mount?"

"What about putting all the Jews in a concentration
camp in Idaho?" said Kimberley.

"What about what-what-what?" I asked in bewilder-
ment. At last, at last, and too late, too late, I understood
that this stupid girl was as dangerous as a cobra. It
would be catastrophic if she spread the word that I was
an anti-Semite, especially with so many Jews, having
interbred with Gentiles, now sending their children to
Tarkington.

"In all my life, I never said anything like that," I
promised.

"Maybe it wasn't Idaho," she said.

"Wyoming?" I said.

"OK, Wyoming," she said. "Lock 'em all up, right?"

"I only said 'Wyoming' because I was married in
Wyoming," I said. "I've never been to Idaho or even
thought about Idaho. I'm just trying to figure out what
you've got so all mixed up and upside down. It doesn't
sound even a little bit like me."

"Jews," she said.

"That was my grandfather again," I said.

"He hated Jews, right?" she said.

"No, no, no," I said. "He admired a lot of them."

"But he still wanted to put them in concentration
camps," she said. "Right?"

The origin of this most poisonous misunderstanding
was in my account in Chapel of riding around with
Grandfather in his car one Sunday morning in Midland
City, Ohio, when I was a little boy. He, not I, was
mocking all organized religions.

When we passed a Catholic church, I recalled, he

said, "You think your dad's a good chemist? They're turning soda crackers into meat in there. Can your dad do that?"

When we passed a Pentecostal church, he said, "The mental giants in there believe that every word is true in a book put together by a bunch of preachers 300 years after the birth of Christ. I hope you won't be that dumb about words set in type when you grow up."

I would later hear, incidentally, that the woman my father got involved with when I was in high school, when he jumped out a window with his pants down and got bitten by a dog and tangled in a clothesline and so on, was a member of that Pentecostal church.

What he said about Jews that morning was actually another kidding of Christianity. He had to explain to me, as I would have to explain to Kimberley, that the Bible consisted of 2 separate works, the New Testament and the Old Testament. Religious Jews gave credence only to what was supposedly their own history, the Old Testament, whereas Christians took both works seriously.

"I pity the Jews," said Grandfather, "trying to get through life with only half a Bible."

And then he added, "That's like trying to get from here to San Francisco with a road map that stops at Dubuque, Iowa."

I was angry now. "Kimberley," I asked, "did you by any chance tell the Board of Trustees that I said these things? Is that what they want to see me about?"

"Maybe," she said. She was acting cute. I thought this was a dumb answer. It was in fact accurate. The

Trustees had a lot more they wanted to discuss than misrepresentations of my Chapel lecture.

I found her both repulsive and pitiful. She thought she was such a heroine and I was such a viper! Now that I had caught on to what she had been up to, she was thrilled to show me that she was proud and unafraid. Little did she know that I had once thrown a man almost as big as she out of a helicopter. What was to prevent me from throwing her out a tower window? The thought of doing that to her crossed my mind. I was so insulted! That would teach her not to insult me!

The man I threw out of the helicopter had spit in my face and bitten my hand. I had taught him not to insult me.

She was pitiful because she was a dimwit from a brilliant family and believed that she at last had done something brilliant, too, in getting the goods on a person whose ideas were criminal. I didn't know yet that her Rhodes Scholar father, a Phi Beta Kappa from Princeton, had put her up to this. I thought she had noted her father's conviction, often expressed in his columns and on his TV show, and no doubt at home, that a few teachers who secretly hated their country were making young people lose faith in its future and leadership.

I thought that, just on her own, she had resolved to find such a villain and get him fired, proving that she wasn't so dumb, after all, and that she was really Daddy's little girl.

Wrong.

"Kimberley," I said, as an alternative to throwing her out the window, "this is ridiculous."

Wrong.

"All right," I said, "we're going to settle this in a hurry."

Wrong.

I would stride into the Trustees' meeting, I thought, shoulders squared, and radiant with righteous indignation, the most popular teacher on campus, and the only faculty member who had medals from the Vietnam War. When it comes right down to it, that is why they fired me, although I don't believe they themselves realized that that was why they fired me: I had ugly, personal knowledge of the disgrace that was the Vietnam War.

None of the Trustees had been in that war, and neither had Kimberley's father, and not one of them had allowed a son or a daughter to be sent over there. Across the lake in the prison, of course, and down in the town, there were plenty of somebody's sons who had been sent over there.

12

I met just 2 people when I crossed the Quadrangle to Samoza Hall. One was Professor Marilyn Shaw, head of the Department of Life Sciences. She was the only other faculty member who had served in Vietnam. She had been a nurse. The other was Norman Everett, an old campus gardener like my grandfather. He had a son who had been paralyzed from the waist down by a mine in Vietnam and was a permanent resident in a Veterans Administration hospital over in Schenectady.

The seniors and their families and the rest of the faculty were having lunch in the Pavilion. Everybody got a lobster which had been boiled alive.

I never considered making a pass at Marilyn, although she was reasonably attractive and unattached. I don't know why that is. There may have been some sort of incest taboo operating, as though we were brother and sister, since we had both been in Vietnam.

She is dead now, buried next to the stable, in the shadow of Musket Mountain when the Sun goes down.

She was evidently hit by a stray bullet. Who in his right mind would have taken dead aim at her?

Remembering her now, I wonder if I wasn't in love with her, even though we avoided talking to each other as much as possible.

Maybe I should put her on a very short list indeed: all the women I loved. That would be Marilyn, I think, and Margaret during the first 4 years or so of our marriage, before I came home with the clap. I was also very fond of Harriet Gummer, the war correspondent for *The Des Moines Register,* who, it turns out, bore me a son after our love affair in Manila. I think I felt what could be called love for Zuzu Johnson, whose husband was crucified. And I had a deep, thoroughly reciprocated, multidimensioned friendship with Muriel Peck, who was a bartender at the Black Cat Café the day I was fired, who later became a member of the English Department.

End of list.

Muriel, too, is buried next to the stable, in the shadow of Musket Mountain when the Sun goes down.

Harriet Gummer is also dead, but out in Iowa.

Hey, girls, wait for me, wait for me.

I don't expect to break a world's record with the number of women I made love to, whether I loved them or not. As far as I am concerned, the record set by Georges Simenon, the French mystery writer, can stand for all time. According to his obituary in *The New York Times,* he copulated with 3 different women a day for years and years.

Marilyn Shaw and I hadn't known each other in Vietnam, but we had a friend in common there, Sam Wakefield. Afterward, he had hired both of us for Tarking-ton, and then committed suicide for reasons unclear even to himself, judging from the plagiarized note he left on his bedside table.

He and his wife, who would become Tarkington's Dean of Women, were sleeping in separate rooms by then.

Sam Wakefield, in my opinion, saved Marilyn's and my lives before he gave up on his own. If he hadn't hired both of us for Tarkington, where we both became very good teachers of the learning-disabled, I don't know what would have become of either of us. When we passed yet again like ships in the night on the Quadran-gle, with me on my way to get fired, I was, incredibly, a tenured Full Professor of Physics and she was a tenured Full Professor of Life Sciences!

When I was still a teacher here, I asked GRIOT™, the most popular computer game at the Pahlavi Pavilion, what might have become of me after the war instead of what really happened. The way you play GRIOT™, of course, is to tell the computer the age and race and degree of education and present situation and drug use, if any, and so on of a person. The person doesn't have to be real. The computer doesn't ask if the person is real or not. It doesn't care about anything. It especially doesn't care about hurting people's feelings. You load it up with details about a life, real or imagined, and then it spits out a story about what was likely to happen to him or her. This story is based on what has happened to real persons with the same general specifications.

GRIOT™ won't work without certain pieces of infor-mation. If you leave out race, for instance, it flashes the words "ethnic origin" on its screen, and stops cold. If it doesn't know that, it can't go on. The same with education.

I didn't tell GRIOT™ that I had landed a job I loved here. I told it only about my life up to the end of the Vietnam War. It knew all about the Vietnam War and the sorts of veterans it had produced. It made me a burned-out case, on the basis of my length of service over there, I think. It had me becoming a wife-beater and an alcoholic, and winding up all alone on Skid Row.

If I had access to GRIOT™ now, I might ask it what might have happened to Marilyn Shaw if Sam Wakefield hadn't rescued her. But the escaped convicts smashed up the one in the Pavilion soon after I showed them how to work it.

They hated it, and I didn't blame them. I was immediately sorry that I had let them know of its existence. One by one they punched in their race and age and what their parents did, if they knew, and how long they'd gone to school and what drugs they'd taken and so on, and GRIOT™ sent them straight to jail to serve long sentences.

I have no idea how much GRIOT™ back then may have known about Vietnam nurses. The manufacturers claimed then as now that no program in stores was more than 3 months old, and so every program was right up-to-date about what had really happened to this or that sort of person at the time you bought it. The programmers, supposedly, were constantly updating GRIOT™ with the news of the day about plumbers, about podiatrists, about Vietnam boat people and Mexican wetbacks, about drug smugglers, about paraplegics, about everyone you could think of within the continental limits of the United States and Canada.

There is some question now, I've heard, about whether GRIOT™ is as deep and up-to-date as it used to be, since Parker Brothers, the company that makes it, has been taken over by Koreans. The new owners are moving the whole operation to Indonesia, where labor costs next to nothing. They say they will keep up with American news by satellite.

One wonders.

I don't need any help from GRIOT™ to know that Marilyn Shaw had a much rougher war than I did. All the soldiers she had to deal with were wounded, and all of them expected of her what was more often than not impossible: that she make them whole again.

I know that she was married, and that her husband back home divorced her and married somebody else while she was still over there, and that she didn't care. She and Sam Wakefield may have been lovers over there. I never asked.

That seems likely. After the war he went looking for her and found her taking a course in Computer Science at New York University. She didn't want to be a nurse anymore. He told her that maybe she should try being a teacher instead. She asked him if there was a chapter of Alcoholics Anonymous in Scipio, and he said there was.

After he shot himself, Marilyn, Professor Shaw, fell off the wagon for about a week. She disappeared, and I was given the job of finding her. I discovered her downtown, drunk and asleep on a pool table in the back room of the Black Cat Café. She was drooling on the felt. One hand was on the cue ball, as though she meant to throw it at something when she regained consciousness.

As far as I know, she never took another drink.

GRIOT™, in the old days anyway, before the Koreans promised to make Parker Brothers lean and mean in Indonesia, didn't come up with the same biography every time you gave it a certain set of facts. Like life itself, it offered a variety of possibilities, spitting out endings according to what the odds for winning or losing or whatever were known to be.

After GRIOT™ put me on Skid Row 15 years ago, I had it try again. I did a little better, but not as well as I was doing here. It had me stay in the Army and become an instructor at West Point, but unhappy and bored. I lost my wife again, and still drank too much, and had a succession of woman friends who soon got sick of me and my depressions. And I died of cirrhosis of the liver a second time.

GRIOT™ didn't have many alternatives to jail for the escaped convicts, though. If it came up with a parole, it soon put the ex-con back in a cage again.

The same thing happened if GRIOT™ was told that the jailbird was Hispanic. It was somewhat more optimistic about Whites, if they could read and write, and had never been in a mental hospital or been given a Dishonorable Discharge from the Armed Forces. Otherwise, they might as well be Black or Hispanic.

The wild cards among jailbirds, as far as GRIOT™ was concerned, were Orientals and American Indians.

When the Supreme Court handed down its decision
that prisoners should be segregated according to race,
many jurisdictions did not have enough Oriental or
American Indian criminals to make separate institutions for them economically feasible. Hawaii, for example, had only 2 American Indian prisoners, and
Wyoming, my wife's home state, had only 1 Oriental.

Under such circumstances, said the Court, Indians
and/or Orientals should be made honorary Whites, and
treated accordingly.

This state has plenty of both, however, particularly
after Indians began to make tax-free fortunes smuggling
drugs over unmapped trails across the border from
Canada. So the Indians had a prison all their own at
what their ancestors used to call "Thunder Beaver,"
what we call "Niagara Falls." The Orientals have their
own prison at Deer Park, Long Island, conveniently
located only 50 kilometers from their heroin-processing
plants in New York City's Chinatown.

When you dare to think about how huge the illegal
drug business is in this country, you have to suspect that
practically everybody has a steady buzz on, just as I did
during my last 2 years in high school, and just as General Grant did during the Civil War, and just as Winston Churchill did during World War II.

So Marilyn Shaw and I passed yet again like ships in
the night on the Quadrangle. It would be our last en-
counter there. Without either of us knowing that it
would be the last time, she said something that in retrospect is quite moving to me. What she said was derived

from our exploratory conversation at the cocktail party that had welcomed us to the faculty so long ago.

I had told her about how I met Sam Wakefield at the Cleveland Science Fair, and what the first words were that he ever spoke to me. Now, as I hastened to my doom, she played back those words to me: "What's the hurry, Son?"

13

The Chairman of the Board of Trustees that fired me 10 years ago was Robert W. Moellenkamp of West Palm Beach, himself a graduate of Tarkington and the father of 2 Tarkingtonians, 1 of whom had been my student. As it happened, he was on the verge of losing his fortune, which was nothing but paper, in Microsecond Arbitrage, Incorporated. That swindle claimed to be snapping up bargains in food and shelter and clothing and fuel and medicine and raw materials and machinery and so on before people who really needed them could learn of their existence. And then the company's computers, supposedly, would get the people who really needed whatever it was to bid against each other, running profits right through the roof. It was able to do this with its clients' money, supposedly, because its computers were linked by satellites to marketplaces in every corner of the world.

The computers, it would turn out, weren't connected to anything but each other and their credulous clients like Tarkington's Board Chairman. He was high as a kite on printouts describing brilliant trades he had made in places like Tierra del Fuego and Uganda and God knows where else, when he agreed with the Panjandrum of American Conservatism, Jason Wilder, that it was time to fire me. Microsecond Arbitrage was his angel dust, his LSD, his heroin, his jug of Thunderbird wine, his cocaine.

I myself have been addicted to older women and housekeeping, which my court-appointed lawyer tells me might be germs we could make grow into a credible plea of insanity. The most amazing thing to him was that I had never masturbated.

"Why not?" he said.

"My mother's father made me promise never to do it, because it would make me lazy and crazy," I said.

"And you believed him?" he said. He is only 23 years old, fresh out of Syracuse.

And I said, "Counselor, in these fast-moving times, with progress gone hog-wild, grandfathers are bound to be wrong about everything."

Robert W. Moellenkamp hadn't heard yet that he and his wife and kids were as broke as any convict in Athena. So when I came into the Board Room back in 1991, he addressed me in the statesmanlike tones of a prudent conservator of a noble legacy. He nodded in the direction of Jason Wilder, who was then simply a Tarkington parent, not a member of the Board. Wilder sat at the opposite end of the great oval table with a manila folder, a tape recorder and cassettes, and a Polaroid photograph deployed before him.

I knew who he was, of course, and something of how his mind worked, having read his newspaper column

and watched his television show from time to time. But
we had not met before. The Board members on either
side of him had crowded into one another in order to
give him plenty of room for some kind of performance.

He was the only celebrity there. He was probably the
only true celebrity ever to set foot in that Board Room.

There was 1 other non-Trustee present. That was the
College President, Henry "Tex" Johnson, whose wife
Zuzu, as I've already said, I used to make love to when
he was away from home any length of time. Zuzu and
I had broken up for good about a month before, but we
were still on speaking terms.

"Please take a seat, Gene," said Moellenkamp. "Mr.
Wilder, who I guess you know is Kimberley's father, has
a rather disturbing story he wants to tell to you."

"I see," I said, a good soldier doing as I was told. I
wanted to keep my job. This was my home. When the
time came, I wanted to retire here and then be buried
here. That was before it was clear that glaciers were
headed south again, and that anybody buried here, including the gang by the stable, along with Musket
Mountain itself, would eventually wind up in Pennsylvania or West Virginia. Or Maryland.

Where else could I become a Full Professor or a
college teacher of any rank, with nothing but a Bachelor
of Science Degree from West Point? I couldn't even
teach high school or grade school, since I had never
taken any of the required courses in education. At my
age, which was then 51, who would hire me for anything, and especially with a demented wife and mother-
in-law in tow.

I said to the Trustees and Jason Wilder, "I believe I
know most of what the story is, ladies and gentlemen.

I've just been with Kimberley, and she gave me a pretty good rehearsal for what I'd better say here.

"When listening to her charges against me, I can only hope you did not lose sight of what you yourselves have learned about me during my 15 years of faithful service to Tarkington. This Board itself, surely, can provide all the character witnesses I could ever need. If not, bring in parents and students. Choose them at random. You know and I know that they will all speak well of me."

I nodded respectfully in Jason Wilder's direction. "I am glad to meet you in person, sir. I read your columns and watch your TV show regularly. I find what you have to say invariably thought-provoking, and so do my wife and her mother, both of them invalids." I wanted to get that in about my 2 sick dependents, in case Wilder and a couple of new Trustees hadn't heard about them.

Actually, I was laying it on pretty thick. Although Margaret and her mother read to each other a lot, taking turns, and usually by flashlight in a tent they'd made inside the house out of bedspreads and chairs or whatever, they never read a newspaper. They didn't like television, either, except for *Sesame Street,* which was supposedly for children. The only time they saw Jason Wilder on the little screen as far as I can remember, my mother-in-law started dancing to him as though he were modern music.

When one of his guests on the show said something, she froze. Only when Wilder spoke did she start to dance again.

I certainly wasn't going to tell him that.

"I want to say first," said Wilder, "that I am in nothing less than awe, Professor Hartke, of your magnificent

record in the Vietnam War. If the American people had
not lost their courage and ceased to support you, we
would be living in a very different and much better
world, and especially in Asia. I know, too, of your
kindness and understanding toward your wife and her
mother, to which I am glad to apply the same encomium
your behavior earned in Vietnam, 'beyond the call of
duty.' So I am sorry to have to warn you that the story
I am about to tell you may not be nearly as simple or
easy to refute as my daughter may have led you to
expect."

"Whatever it is, sir," I said, "let's hear it. Shoot."

So he did. He said that several of his friends had
attended Tarkington or sent their children here, so that
he was favorably impressed with the institution's successes with the learning-disabled long before he en-
trusted his own daughter to us. An usher and a
bridesmaid at his wedding, he said, had earned Associate in the Arts and Sciences Degrees in Scipio. The
usher had gone on to be Ambassador to Iceland. The
bridesmaid was on the Board of Directors of the Chicago Symphony Orchestra.

He felt that Tarkington's highly unconventional tech-
niques would be useful if applied to the country's
notoriously beleaguered inner-city schools, and he
planned to say so after he had learned more about them.
The ratio of teachers to students at Tarkington, incidentally, was then 1 to 6. In inner-city schools, that ratio
was then 1 to 65.

There was a big campaign back then, I remember, to
get the Japanese to buy up inner-city public schools the
way they were buying up prisons and hospitals. But they
were too smart. They wouldn't touch schools for unwel-

come children of unwelcome parents with a 10-foot
pole.

He said he hoped to write a book about Tarkington
called "Little Miracle on Lake Mohiga" or "Teaching
the Unteachable." So he wired his daughter for sound
and told her to follow the best teachers in order to
record what they said and how they said it. "I wanted
to learn what it was that made them good, Professor
Hartke, without their knowing they were being stud-
ied," he said. "I wanted them to go on being whatever
they were, warts and all, without any self-conscious-
ness."

This was the first I heard of the tapes. That chilling
news explained Kimberley's lurking, lurking, lurking all
the time. Wilder spared me the suspense, at least, of
wondering what all of Kimberley's apparatus might
have overheard. He punched the playback button on
the recorder before him, and I heard myself telling Paul
Slazinger, privately, I'd thought, that the two principal
currencies of the planet were the Yen and fellatio. This
was so early in the academic year that classes hadn't
begun yet! This was during Freshman Orientation
Week, and I had just told the incoming Class of 1994
that merchants and tradespeople in the town below preferred to be paid in Japanese Yen rather than dollars, so
that the freshmen might want their parents to give them
their allowances in Yen.

I had told them, too, that they were never to go into
the Black Cat Café, which the townspeople considered
their private club. It was one place they could go and
not be reminded of how dependent they were on the rich
kids on the hill, but I didn't say that. Neither did I say
that free-lance prostitutes were sometimes found there,

and in the past had been the cause of outbreaks of venereal disease on campus.

I had kept it simple for the freshmen: "Tarkingtonians are more than welcome anywhere in town but the Black Cat Café."

If Kimberley recorded that good advice, her father did not play it back for me. He didn't even play back what Slazinger had said to me, and it was during a coffee break, that stimulated me to name the planet's two most acceptable currencies. He was the agent provocateur.

What he said, as I recall, was, "They want to get paid in Yen?" He was as new to Scipio as any freshman, and we had just met. I hadn't read any of his books, and so far as I knew, neither had anybody else on the faculty. He was a last-minute choice for Writer in Residence, and had come to orientation because he was lonesome and had nothing else to do. He wasn't supposed to be there, and he was so old, so old! He had been sitting among all those teenagers as though he were just another rich kid who had bottomed out on his Scholastic Aptitude Test, and he was old enough to be their grandfather!

He had fought in World War II! That's how old he was.

So I said to him, "They'll take dollars if they have to, but you'd better have a wheelbarrow."

And he wanted to know if the merchants and tradespeople would also accept fellatio. He used a vernacular word for fellatio in the plural.

But the tape began right after that, with my saying, as though out of the blue, and as a joke, of course, only it didn't sound like a joke during the playback, that, in effect, the whole World was for sale to anyone who had Yen or was willing to perform fellatio.

14

So that was twice within an hour that I was accused of cynicism that was Paul Slazinger's, not mine. And he was in Key West, well out of reach of punishment, having been unemployment-proofed for 5 years with a Genius Grant from the MacArthur Foundation. In saying what I had about Yen and fellatio, I was being sociable with a stranger. I was echoing him to make him feel at home in new surroundings.

As far as that goes, Professor Damon Stern, head of the History Department and my closest male friend here, spoke as badly of his own country as Slazinger and I did, and right into the faces of students in the classroom day after day. I used to sit in on his course and laugh and clap. The truth can be very funny in an awful way, especially as it relates to greed and hypocrisy. Kimberley must have made recordings of his words, too, and played them back for her father. Why wasn't Damon fired right along with me?

My guess is that he was a comedian, and I was not. He wanted students to leave his presence feeling good, not bad, so the atrocities and stupidities he described were in the distant past. There was nothing a student could do about them but laugh, laugh, laugh.

Whereas Slazinger and I talked about the last half of the 20th Century, in which we had both been seriously wounded physically and psychologically, which was nothing anybody but a sociopath could laugh about.

I, too, might have been acceptable as a comedian if all Kimberley had taped was what I said about Yen and fellatio. That was good, topical Mohiga Valley humor, what with the Japanese taking over the prison across the lake and arousing curiosity among the natives about the relative values of different national currencies. The Japanese were willing to pay their local bills in either dollars or Yen. These bills were for small-ticket items, hardware or toiletries or whatever, which the prison needed in a hurry, usually ordered by telephone. Big-ticket items in quantity came from Japanese-owned suppliers in Rochester or beyond.

So Japanese currency had started to circulate in Scipio. The prison administrators and guards were rarely seen in town, however. They lived in barracks to the east of the prison, and lived lives as invisible to this side of the lake as those of the prisoners.

To the limited extent that anybody on this side of the lake thought about the prison at all until the mass escape, people were generally glad to have the Japanese in charge. The new proprietor had cut waste and corruption to almost nothing. What they charged the State for punishing its prisoners was only 75 percent of what the State used to pay itself for identical services.

The local paper, *The Valley Sentinel*, sent a reporter

over there to see what the Japanese were doing differently. They were still using the steel boxes on the back of trucks and showing old TV shows, including news, in no particular order and around the clock. The biggest change was that Athena was drug-free for the first time in its history, and rich prisoners weren't able to buy privileges. The guards weren't easily fooled or corrupted, either, since they understood so little English, and wanted nothing more than to finish up their 6 months overseas and go home again.

A normal tour of duty in Vietnam was twice that long and 1,000 times more dangerous. Who could blame the educated classes with political connections for staying home?

One new wrinkle by the Japanese the reporter didn't mention was that the guards wore surgical masks and rubber gloves when they were on duty, even up in the towers and atop the walls. That wasn't to keep them from spreading infections, of course. It was to ensure that they didn't take any of their loathsome charges' loathsome diseases back home with them.

When I went to work over there, I refused to wear gloves and a mask. Who could teach anybody anything while wearing such a costume?
So now I have tuberculosis.
Cough, cough, cough.

Before I could protest to the Trustees that I certainly wouldn't have said what I'd said about Yen and fellatio if I'd thought there was the slightest chance that a student could hear me, the background noises on the tape

changed. I realized that I was about to hear something
I had said in a different location. There was the pop-
pop-pop of Ping-Pong balls, and a card player asked,
"Who dealt this mess?" Somebody else asked somebody
else to bring her a hot fudge sundae without nuts on
top. She was on a diet, she said. There were rumblings
like distant artillery, which were really the sound of
bowling balls in the basement of the Pahlavi Pavilion.

Oh Lordy, was I ever drunk that night at the Pavilion.
I was out of control. And it was a disgrace that I should
have appeared before students in such a condition. I will
regret it to my dying day. Cough.

It was on a cold night near the end of November of
1990, 6 months before the Trustees fired me. I know it
wasn't December, because Slazinger was still on campus, talking openly of suicide. He hadn't yet received his
Genius Grant.

When I came home from work that afternoon, to tidy
up the house and make supper, I found an awful mess.
Margaret and Mildred, both hags by then, had torn
bedsheets into strips. I had laundered the sheets that
morning, and was going to put them on our beds that
night. What did they care?

They had constructed what they said was a spider
web. At least it wasn't a hydrogen bomb.

White cotton strips spliced end to end crisscrossed
every which way in the front hall and living room. The
newel post of the stairway was connected to the inside
doorknob of the front door, and the doorknob was
connected to the living room chandelier, and so on ad
infinitum.

The day hadn't begun auspiciously anyway. I had found all 4 tires of my Mercedes flat. A bunch of high school kids from down below, high on alcohol or who knows what, had come up during the night like Vietcong and gone what they called "coring" again. They not only had let the air out of the tires of every expensive car they could find in the open on campus, Porsches and Jaguars and Saabs and BMWs and so on, but had taken out the valve cores. At home, I had heard, they had jars full of valve cores or necklaces of valve cores to prove how often they had gone coring. And they got my Mercedes. They got my Mercedes every time.

So when I found myself tangled in Margaret and Mildred's spider web, my nervous system came close to the breaking point. I was the one who was going to have to clean up this mess. I was the one who was going to have to remake the beds with other sheets, and then buy more sheets the next day. I have always liked housework, or at least not minded it as much as most people seem to. But this was housework beyond the pale!

I had left the house so neat in the morning! And Margaret and Mildred weren't getting any fun out of watching my reactions when I was tangled up in their spider web. They were hiding someplace where they couldn't see or hear me. They expected me to play hide-and-seek, with me as "it."

Something in me snapped. I wasn't going to play hide-and-seek this time. I wasn't going to take down the spider web. I wasn't going to prepare supper. Let them come creeping out of their hiding places in an hour or whatever. Let them wonder, as I had when I walked into the spider web, what on Earth had happened to their previously dependable, forgiving Universe?

Out into the cold night I went, with no destination in mind save for good old oblivion. I found myself in front of the house of my best friend, Damon Stern, the entertaining professor of History. When he was a boy in Wisconsin, he had learned how to ride a unicycle. He had taught his wife and kids how to ride one, too.

The lights were on, but nobody was home. The family's 4 unicycles were in the front hall and the car was gone. They never got cored. They were smart. They drove one of the last Volkswagen Bugs still running.

I knew where they kept the liquor. I poured myself a couple of stiff shots of bourbon, in lieu of their absent body warmth. I don't think I had had a drink for a month before that.

I got this hot rush in my belly. Out into the night I went again. I was automatically looking for an older woman who would make everything all right by becoming the beast with two backs with me.

A coed would not do, not that a coed would have had anything to do with somebody as old and relatively poor as me. I couldn't even have promised her a better grade than she deserved. There were no grades at Tarkington.

But I wouldn't have wanted a coed in any case. The only sort of woman who excites me is an older one in uncomfortable circumstances, full of doubts not only about herself but about the value of life itself. Although I never met her personally, the late Marilyn Monroe comes to mind, maybe 3 years before she committed suicide.

Cough, cough, cough.

If there is a Divine Providence, there is also a wicked one, provided you agree that making love to off-balance women you aren't married to is wickedness. My own feeling is that if adultery is wickedness then so is food. Both make me feel so much better afterward.

Just as a hungry person knows that somewhere not far away somebody is preparing good things to eat, I knew that night that not far away was an older woman in despair. There had to be!

Zuzu Johnson was out of the question. Her husband was home, and she was hosting a dinner party for a couple of grateful parents who were giving the college a language laboratory. When it was finished, students would be able to sit in soundproof booths and listen to recordings of any one of more than 100 languages and dialects made by native speakers.

The lights were on in the sculpture studio of Norman Rockwell Hall, the art building, the only structure on campus named after a historical figure rather than the donating family. It was another gift from the Moellen-kamps, who may have felt that too much was named after them already.

There was a whirring and rumbling coming from inside the sculpture studio. Somebody was playing with the crane in there, making it run back and forth on its tracks overhead. Whoever it was had to be playing, since nobody ever made a piece of sculpture so big that it could be moved only by the mighty crane.

After the prison break, there was some talk on the part of the convicts of hanging somebody from it, and running him back and forth while he strangled. They had no particular candidate in mind. But then the

Niagara Power and Light Company, which was owned
by the Unification Church Korean Evangelical Associa-
tion, shut off all our electricity.

Outside Rockwell Hall that night, I might have been
back on a patrol in Vietnam. That is how keen my
senses were. That was how quick my mind was to create
a whoie picture from the slightest clues.

I knew that the sculpture studio was locked up tight
after 6:30 P.M., since I had tried the door many times,
thinking that I might sometime bring a lover there. I
had considered getting a key somehow at the start of the
semester and learned from Buildings and Grounds that
only they and that year's Artist in Residence, the sculp-
tress Pamela Ford Hall, were allowed to have keys. This
was because of vandalism by either students or Townies
in the studio the year before.

They knocked off the noses and fingers of replicas of
Greek statues, and defecated in a bucket of wet clay.
That sort of thing.

So that had to be Pamela Ford Hall in there making
the crane go back and forth. And the crane's restless
travels had to represent unhappiness, not any master-
piece she was creating. What use did she have for a
crane, or even a wheelbarrow, since she worked exclu-
sively in nearly weightless polyurethane. And she was a
recent divorcée without children. And, because she
knew my reputation, I'm sure, she had been avoiding
me.

I climbed up on the studio's loading dock. I thumped
my fist on its enormous sliding door. The door was
motor driven. She had only to press a button to let me
in.

The crane stopped going back and forth. There was a hopeful sign!

She asked through the door what I wanted.

"I wanted to make sure you were OK in there," I said.

"Who are you to care whether I'm OK or not in here?" she said.

"Gene Hartke," I said.

She opened the door just a crack and stared out at me, but didn't say anything. Then she opened the door wider, and I could see she was holding an uncorked bottle of what would turn out to be blackberry brandy.

"Hello, Soldier," she said.

"Hi," I said very carefully.

And then she said, "What took you so long?"

15

Pamela sure got me drunk that night, and we made love. And then I spilled my guts about the Vietnam War in front of a bunch of students at the Pahlavi Pavilion. And Kimberley Wilder recorded me.

I had never tasted blackberry brandy before. I never want to taste it again. It did bad things to me. It made me a crybaby about the war. That is something I swore I would never be.

If I could order any drink I wanted now, it would be a Sweet Rob Roy on the Rocks, a Manhattan made with Scotch. That was another drink a woman introduced me to, and it made me laugh instead of cry, and fall in love with the woman who said to try one.

That was in Manila, after the excrement hit the air-conditioning in Saigon. She was Harriet Gummer, the war correspondent from Iowa. She had a son by me without telling me.

His name? Rob Roy.

After we made love, Pamela asked me the same question Harriet had asked me in Manila 15 years earlier. It was something they both had to know. They both asked me if I had killed anybody in the war.

I said to Pamela what I had said to Harriet: "If I were a fighter plane instead of a human being, there would be little pictures of people painted all over me."

I should have gone straight home after saying that. But I went over to the Pavilion instead. I needed a bigger audience for that great line of mine.

So I barged into a group of students sitting in front of the great fireplace in the main lounge. After the prison break, that fireplace would be used for cooking horse meat and dogs. I got between the students and the fire, so there was no way they could ignore me, and I said to them, "If I were a fighter plane instead of a human being, there would be little pictures of people painted all over me."

I went on from there.

I was so full of self-pity! That was what I found unbearable when Jason Wilder played back my words to me. I was so drunk that I acted like a victim!

The scenes of unspeakable cruelty and stupidity and waste I described that night were no more horrible than ultrarealistic shows about Vietnam, which had become staples of TV entertainment. When I told the students about the severed human head I saw nestled in the guts of a water buffalo, to them, I'm sure, the head might as well have been made of wax, and the guts those of some big animal which may or may not have belonged to a real water buffalo.

What difference could it make whether the head was or was not wax, or whether the guts were or were not those of a water buffalo?

No difference.

"Professor Hartke," Jason Wilder said to me gently, reasonably, when the tape had reached its end, "why on Earth would you want to tell such tales to young people who need to love their country?"

I wanted to keep my job so much, and the house which came with it, that my reply was asinine. "I was telling them history," I said, "and I had had a little too much to drink. I don't usually drink that much."

"I'm sure," he said. "I am told that you are a man with many problems, but that alcohol has not appeared among them with any consistency. So let us say that your performance in the Pavilion was a well-intended history lesson of which you accidentally lost control."

"That's what it was, sir," I said.

His balletic hands flitted in time to the logic of his thoughts before he spoke again. He was a fellow pianist. And then he said, "First of all, you were not hired to teach History. Second of all, the students who come to Tarkington need no further instructions in how it feels to be defeated. They would not be here if they themselves had not failed and failed. The Miracle on Lake Mohiga for more than a century now, as I see it, has been to make children who have failed and failed start thinking of victory, stop thinking about the hopelessness of it all."

"There was just that one time," I said, "and I'm sorry."

Cough. One cough.

Wilder said he didn't consider a teacher who was negative about everything a teacher. "I would call a person like that an 'unteacher.' He's somebody who takes things out of young people's heads instead of putting more things in."

"I don't know as I'm negative about everything," I said.

"What's the first thing students see when they walk into the library?" he said.

"Books?" I said.

"All those perpetual-motion machines," he said. "I saw that display, and I read the sign on the wall above it. I had no idea then that you were responsible for the sign."

He was talking about the sign that said "THE COMPLICATED FUTILITY OF IGNORANCE."

"All I knew was that I didn't want my daughter or anybody's child to see a message that negative every time she comes into the library," he said. "And then I found out it was you who was responsible for it."

"What's so negative about it?" I said.

"What could be a more negative word than 'futility'?" he said.

" 'Ignorance,' " I said.

"There you are," he said. I had somehow won his argument for him.

"I don't understand," I said.

"Precisely," he said. "You obviously do not understand how easily discouraged the typical Tarkington student is, how sensitive to suggestions that he or she should quit trying to be smart. That's what the word 'futile' means: 'Quit, quit, quit.' "

"And what does 'ignorance' mean?" I said.

"If you put it up on the wall and give it the prominence you have," he said, "it's a nasty echo of what so many Tarkingtonians were hearing before they got here: 'You're dumb, you're dumb, you're dumb.' And of course they aren't dumb."

"I never said they were," I protested.

"You reinforce their low self-esteem without realizing what you are doing," he said. "You also upset them with humor appropriate to a barracks, but certainly not to an institution of higher learning."

"You mean about Yen and fellatio?" I said. "I would never have said it if I'd thought a student could hear me."

"I am talking about the entrance hall of the library again," he said.

"I can't think of what else is in there that might have offended you," I said.

"It wasn't I who was offended," he said. "It was my daughter."

"I give up," I said. I wasn't being impudent. I was abject.

"On the same day Kimberley heard you talk about Yen and fellatio, before classes had even begun," he said, "a senior led her and the other freshmen to the library and solemnly told them that the bell clappers on the wall were petrified penises. That was surely barracks humor the senior had picked up from you."

For once I didn't have to defend myself. Several of the Trustees assured Wilder that telling freshmen that the clappers were penises was a tradition that antedated my arrival on campus by at least 20 years.

But that was the only time they defended me, although 1 of them had been my student, Madelaine Astor, née Peabody, and 5 of them were parents of those I had taught. Madelaine dictated a letter to me

afterward, explaining that Jason Wilder had promised
to denounce the college in his column and on his TV
show if the Trustees did not fire me.

So they dared not come to my assistance.

She said, too, that since she, like Wilder, was a
Roman Catholic, she was shocked to hear me say on
tape that Hitler was a Roman Catholic, and that the
Nazis painted crosses on their tanks and airplanes because they considered themselves a Christian army.
Wilder had played that tape right after I had been
cleared of all responsibility for freshmen's being told
that the clappers were penises.

Once again I was in deep trouble for merely repeating
what somebody else had said. It wasn't something my
grandfather had said this time, or somebody else who
couldn't be hurt by the Trustees, like Paul Slazinger. It
was something my best friend Damon Stern had said in
a History class only a couple of months before.

If Jason Wilder thought I was an unteacher, he
should have heard Damon Stern! Then again, Stern
never told the awful truth about supposedly noble
human actions in recent times. Everything he debunked
had to have transpired before 1950, say.

So I happened to sit in on a class where he talked
about Hitler's being a devout Roman Catholic. He said
something I hadn't realized before, something I have
since discovered most Christians don't want to hear:
that the Nazi swastika was intended to be a version of
a Christian cross, a cross made out of axes. Stern said
that Christians had gone to a lot of trouble denying that
the swastika was just another cross, saying it was a
primitive symbol from the primordial ooze of the pagan
past.

And the Nazis' most valuable military decoration was the Iron Cross.

And the Nazis painted regular crosses on all their tanks and airplanes.

I came out of that class looking sort of dazed, I guess. Who should I run into but Kimberley Wilder?

"What did he say today?" she said.

"Hitler was a Christian," I said. "The swastika was a Christian cross."

She got it on tape.

I didn't rat on Damon Stern to the Trustees. Tarkington wasn't West Point, where it was an honor to squeal.

Madelaine agreed with Wilder, too, she said in her letter, that I should not have told my Physics students that the Russians, not the Americans, were the first to make a hydrogen bomb that was portable enough to be used as a weapon. "Even if it's true," she wrote, "which I don't believe, you had no business telling them that."

She said, moreover, that perpetual motion was possible, if only scientists would work harder on it.

She had certainly backslid intellectually since passing her orals for her Associate in the Arts and Sciences Degree.

I used to tell classes that anybody who believed in the possibility of perpetual motion should be boiled alive like a lobster.

I was also a stickler about the Metric System. I was famous for turning my back on students who mentioned feet or pounds or miles to me.

They hated that.

I didn't dare teach like that in the prison across the lake, of course.

Then again, most of the convicts had been in the drug business, and were either Third World people or dealt with Third World people. So the Metric System was old stuff to them.

Rather than rat on Damon Stern about the Nazis' being Christians, I told the Trustees that I had heard it on National Public Radio. I said I was very sorry about having passed it on to a student. "I feel like biting off my tongue," I said.

"What does Hitler have to do with either Physics or Music Appreciation?" said Wilder.

I might have replied that Hitler probably didn't know any more about physics than the Board of Trustees, but that he loved music. Every time a concert hall was bombed, I heard somewhere, he had it rebuilt immediately as a matter of top priority. I think I may actually have learned that from National Public Radio.

I said instead, "If I'd known I upset Kimberley as much as you say I did, I would certainly have apologized. I had no idea, sir. She gave no sign."

What made me weak was the realization that I had been mistaken to think that I was with family there in the Board Room, that all Tarkingtonians and their parents and guardians had come to regard me as an uncle. My goodness—the family secrets I had learned over the years and kept to myself! My lips were sealed. What a faithful old retainer I was! But that was all I was to the Trustees, and probably to the students, too.

I wasn't an uncle. I was a member of the Servant Class.

They were letting me go.

Soldiers are discharged. People in the workplace are fired. Servants are let go.

"Am I being fired?" I asked the Chairman of the Board incredulously.

"I'm sorry, Gene," he said, "but we're going to have to let you go."

The President of the college, Tex Johnson, sitting two chairs away from me, hadn't let out a peep. He looked sick. I surmised mistakenly that he had been scolded for having let me stay on the faculty long enough to get tenure. He was sick about something more personal, which still had a lot to do with Professor Eugene Debs Hartke.

He had been brought in as President from Rollins College down in Winter Park, Florida, where he had been Provost, after Sam Wakefield did the big trick of suicide. Henry "Tex" Johnson held a Bachelor's Degree in Business Administration from Texas Tech in Lubbock, and claimed to be a descendant of a man who had died in the Alamo. Damon Stern, who was always turning up little-known facts of history, told me, incidentally, that the Battle of the Alamo was about slavery. The brave men who died there wanted to secede from Mexico because it was against the law to own slaves in Mexico. They were fighting for the right to own slaves.

Since Tex's wife and I had been lovers, I knew that his ancestors weren't Texans, but Lithuanians. His father, whose name certainly wasn't Johnson, was a Lithuanian second mate on a Russian freighter who jumped ship when it put in for emergency repairs at Corpus Christi. Zuzu told me that Tex's father was not only an illegal immigrant but the nephew of the former Communist boss of Lithuania.

So much for the Alamo.

I turned to him at the Board meeting, and I said, "Tex—for pity sakes, say something! You know darn good and well I'm the best teacher you've got! I don't say that. The students do! Is the whole faculty going to be brought before this Board, or am I the only one? Tex?"

He stared straight ahead. He seemed to have turned to cement. "Tex?" Some leadership!

I put the same question to the Chairman, who had been pauperized by Microsecond Arbitrage but didn't know it yet. "Bob—" I began.

He winced.

I began again, having gotten the message in spades that I was a servant and not a relative: "Mr. Moellenkamp, sir—" I said, "you know darn well, and so does everybody else here, that you can follow the most patriotic, deeply religious American who ever lived with a tape recorder for a year, and then prove that he's a worse traitor than Benedict Arnold, and a worshipper of the Devil. Who doesn't say things in a moment of passion or absentmindedness that he doesn't wish he could take back? So I ask again, am I the only one this was done to, and if so, why?"

He froze.

"Madelaine?" I said to Madelaine Astor, who would later write me such a dumb letter.

She said she did not like it that I had told students that a new Ice Age was on its way, even if I had read it in *The New York Times*. That was another thing I'd said that Wilder had on tape. At least it had something to do

with science, and at least it wasn't something I had
picked up from Slazinger or Grandfather Wills or
Damon Stern. At least it was the real me.

"The students here have enough to worry about," she
said. "I know I did."

She went on to say that there had always been people
who had tried to become famous by saying that the
World was going to end, but the World hadn't ended.

There were nods of agreement all around the table. I
don't think there was a soul there who knew anything
about science.

"When I was here you were predicting the end of the
World," she said, "only it was atomic waste and acid
rain that were going to kill us. But here we are. I feel
fine. Doesn't everybody else feel fine? So pooh."

She shrugged. "About the rest of it," she said, "I'm
sorry I heard about it. It made me sick. If we have to go
over it again, I think I'll just leave the room."

Heavens to Betsy! What could she have meant by
"the rest of it"? What could it be that they had gone
over once, and were going to have to go over again with
me there? Hadn't I already heard the worst?

No.

16

"The rest of it" was in a manila folder in front of Jason Wilder. So there is Manila playing a big part in my life again. No Sweet Rob Roys on the Rocks this time.

In the folder was a report by a private detective hired by Wilder to investigate my sex life. It covered only the second semester, and so missed the episode in the sculpture studio. The gumshoe recorded 3 of 7 subsequent trysts with the Artist in Residence, 2 with a woman from a jewelry company taking orders for class rings, and maybe 30 with Zuzu Johnson, the wife of the President. He didn't miss a thing Zuzu and I did during the second semester. There was only 1 misunderstood incident: when I went up into the loft of the stable, where the Lutz Carillon had been stored before there was a tower and where Tex Johnson was crucified 2 years ago. I went up with the aunt of a student. She was an architect who wanted to see the pegged post-and-beam joinery up there. The operative assumed we made love up there. We hadn't.

135

We made love much later that afternoon, in a toolshed by the stable, in the shadow of Musket Mountain when the Sun goes down.

I wasn't to see the contents of Wilder's folder for another 10 minutes or so. Wilder and a couple of others wanted to go on discussing what really bothered them about me, which was what I had been doing, supposedly, to the students' minds. My sexual promiscuity among older women wasn't of much interest to them, the College President excepted, save as a handy something for which I could be fired without raising the gummy question of whether or not my rights under the First Amendment of the Constitution had been violated.

Adultery was the bullet they would put in my brain, so to speak, after I had been turned to Swiss cheese by the firing squad.

To Tex Johnson, the closet Lithuanian, the contents of the folder were more than a gadget for diddling me out of tenure. They were a worse humiliation for Tex than they were for me.

At least they said that my love affair with his wife was over.

He stood up. He asked to be excused. He said that he would just as soon not be present when the Trustees went over for the second time what Madelaine had called "the rest of it."

He was excused, and was apparently about to leave without saying anything. But then, with one hand on the doorknob, he uttered two words chokingly, which were the title of a novel by Gustave Flaubert. It was about a wife who was bored with her husband, who had an exceedingly silly love affair and then committed suicide.

"*Madame Bovary,*" he said. And then he was gone.

He was a cuckold in the present, and crucifixion awaited him in the future. I wonder if his father would have jumped ship in Corpus Christi if he had known what an unhappy end his only son would come to under American Free Enterprise.

I had read *Madame Bovary* at West Point. All cadets in my day had to read it, so that we could demonstrate to cultivated people that we, too, were cultivated, should we ever face that challenge. Jack Patton and I read it at the same time for the same class. I asked him afterward what he thought of it. Predictably, he said he had to laugh like hell.

He said the same thing about *Othello* and *Hamlet* and *Romeo and Juliet.*

I confess that to this day I have come to no firm conclusions about how smart or dumb Jack Patton really was. This leaves me in doubt about the meaning of a birthday present he sent me in Vietnam shortly before the sniper killed him with a beautiful shot in Hué, pronounced "whay." It was a gift-wrapped copy of a stroke magazine called *Black Garterbelt.* But did he send it to me for its pictures of women naked except for black garterbelts, or for a remarkable science fiction story in there, "The Protocols of the Elders of Tralfamadore"?

But more about that later.

I have no idea how many of the Trustees had read *Madame Bovary.* Two of them would have had to have it read aloud to them. So I was not alone in wondering why Tex Johnson would have said, his hand on the doorknob, *"Madame Bovary."*

If I had been Tex, I think I might have gotten off the campus as fast as possible, and maybe drowned my sorrows among the nonacademics at the Black Cat Café. That was where I was going to wind up that afternoon. It would have been funny in retrospect if we had wound up as a couple of sloshed buddies at the Black Cat Café.

Imagine my saying to him or his saying to me, both of us drunk as skunks, "I love you, you old son of a gun. Do you know that?"

One Trustee had it in for me on personal grounds. That was Sydney Stone, who was said to have amassed a fortune of more than $1,000,000,000 in 10 short years, mainly in commissions for arranging sales of American properties to foreigners. His masterpiece, maybe, was the transfer of ownership of my father's former employer, E. I. Du Pont de Nemours & Company, to I. G. Farben in Germany.

"There is much I could probably forgive, if somebody put a gun to my head, Professor Hartke," he said, "but not what you did to my son." He himself was no Tarkingtonian. He was a graduate of the Harvard Business School and the London School of Economics.

"Fred?" I said.

"In case you haven't noticed," he said, "I have only 1 son in Tarkington. I have only 1 son anywhere." Presumably this 1 son, without having to lift a finger, would himself 1 day have $1,000,000,000.

"What did I do to Fred?" I said.

"You know what you did to Fred," he said.

What I had done to Fred was catch him stealing a Tarkington beer mug from the college bookstore. What Fred Stone did was beyond mere stealing. He took the beer mug off the shelf, drank make-believe toasts to me and the cashier, who were the only other people there, and then walked out.

I had just come from a faculty meeting where the campus theft problem had been discussed for the umpteenth time. The manager of the bookstore told us that only one comparable institution had a higher percentage of its merchandise stolen than his, which was the Harvard Coop in Cambridge.

So I followed Fred Stone out to the Quadrangle. He was headed for his Kawasaki motorcycle in the student parking lot. I came up behind him and said quietly, with all possible politeness, "I think you should put that beer mug back where you got it, Fred. Either that or pay for it."

"Oh, yeah?" he said. "Is that what you think?" Then he smashed the mug to smithereens on the rim of the Vonnegut Memorial Fountain. "If that's what you think," he said, "then you're the one who should put it back."

I reported the incident to Tex Johnson, who told me to forget it.

But I was mad. So I wrote a letter about it to the boy's father, but never got an answer until the Board meeting.

"I can never forgive you for accusing my son of theft," the father said. He quoted Shakespeare on behalf of Fred. I was supposed to imagine Fred's saying it to me.

" 'Who steals my purse steals trash; 'tis something, nothing,' " he said. " ' 'Twas mine, 'tis his, and has been slave to thousands,' " he went on, " 'but he that filches from me my good name robs me of that which not enriches him and makes me poor indeed.' "

"If I was wrong, sir, I apologize," I said.

"Too late," he said.

17

There was 1 Trustee I was sure was my friend. He would have found what I said on tape funny and interesting. But he wasn't there. His name was Ed Bergeron, and we had had a lot of good talks about the deterioration of the environment and the abuses of trust in the stock market and the banking industry and so on. He could top me for pessimism any day.

His wealth was as old as the Moellenkamps', and was based on ancestral oil fields and coal mines and railroads which he had sold to foreigners in order to devote himself full-time to nature study and conservation. He was President of the Wildlife Rescue Federation, and his photographs of wildlife on the Galápagos Islands had been published in *National Geographic.* The magazine gave him the cover, too, which showed a marine iguana digesting seaweed in the sunshine, right next to a skinny penguin who was no doubt having thoughts about entirely different issues of the day, whatever was going on that day.

Not only was Ed Bergeron my doomsday pal. He was

also a veteran of several debates about environmental-
ism with Jason Wilder on Wilder's TV show. I haven't
found a tape of any of those ding-dong head-to-heads in
this library, but there used to be 1 at the prison. It would
bob up about every 6 months on the TV sets there,
which were running all the time.

In it, I remember, Wilder said that the trouble with
conservationists was that they never considered the
costs in terms of jobs and living standards of eliminat-
ing fossil fuels or doing something with garbage other
than dumping it in the ocean, and so on.

Ed Bergeron said to him, "Good! Then I can write
the epitaph for this once salubrious blue-green orb." He
meant the planet.

Wilder gave him his supercilious, vulpine, patroniz-
ing, silky debater's grin. "A majority of the scientific
community," he said, "would say, if I'm not mistaken,
that an epitaph would be premature by several thousand years." That debate took place maybe 6 years
before I was fired, which would be back in 1985, and I
don't know what scientific community he was talking
about. Every kind of scientist, all the way down to
chiropractors and podiatrists, was saying we were killing the planet fast.

"You want to hear the epitaph?" said Ed Bergeron.

"If we must," said Wilder, and the grin went on and
on. "I have to tell you, though, that you are not the first
person to say the game was all over for the human race.
I'm sure that even in Egypt before the first pyramid was
constructed, there were men who attracted a following
by saying, 'It's all over now.' "

"What is different about now as compared with
Egypt before the first pyramid was built—" Ed began.

"And before the Chinese invented printing, and

before Columbus discovered America," Jason Wilder interjected.

"Exactly," said Bergeron.

"The difference is that we have the misfortune of knowing what's really going on," said Bergeron, "which is no fun at all. And this has given rise to a whole new class of preening, narcissistic quacks like yourself who say in the service of rich and shameless polluters that the state of the atmosphere and the water and the topsoil on which all life depends is as debatable as how many angels can dance on the fuzz of a tennis ball."

He was angry.

When this old tape was played at Athena before the great escape, it kindled considerable interest. I watched it and listened with several students of mine. Afterward one of them said to me, "Who right, Professor—beard or mustache?" Wilder had a mustache. Bergeron had a beard.

"Beard," I said.

That may have been almost the last word I said to a convict before the prison break, before my mother-in-law decided that it was at last time to talk about her big pickerel.

Bergeron's epitaph for the planet, I remember, which he said should be carved in big letters in a wall of the Grand Canyon for the flying-saucer people to find, was this:

WE COULD HAVE SAVED IT,
BUT WE WERE TOO DOGGONE CHEAP.

Only he didn't say "doggone."

But I would never see or hear from Ed Bergeron
again. He resigned from the Board soon after I was
fired, and so would miss being taken hostage by the
convicts. It would have been interesting to hear what he
had to say to and about that particular kind of captor.
One thing he used to say to me, and to a class of mine
he spoke to one time, was that man was the weather
now. Man was the tornadoes, man was the hailstones,
man was the floods. So he might have said that Scipio
was Pompeii, and the escapees were a lava flow.

He didn't resign from the Board on account of my
firing. He had at least two personal tragedies, one right
on top of the other. A company he inherited made all
sorts of products out of asbestos, whose dust proved to
be as carcinogenic as any substance yet identified, with
the exception of epoxy cement and some of the radioactive stuff accidentally turned loose in the air and aquifers around nuclear weapons factories and power
plants. He felt terrible about this, he told me, although
he had never laid eyes on any of the factories that made
the stuff. He sold them for practically nothing, since the
company in Singapore that bought them got all the
lawsuits along with the machinery and buildings, and an
inventory of finished materials which was huge and un-
salable in this country. The people in Singapore did
what Ed couldn't bring himself to do, which was to sell
all those floor tiles and roofing and so on to emerging
nations in Africa.

And then his son Bruce, Tarkington Class of '85, who
was a homosexual, joined the Ice Capades as a chorus
boy. That was all right with Ed, who understood that
some people were born homosexual and that was that.

And Bruce was so happy with the ice show. He was not only a good skater but maybe the best male or female dancer at Tarkington. Bruce used to come over to the house and dance with my mother-in-law sometimes, just for the sake of dancing. He said she was the best dance partner he had ever had, and she returned the compliment.

I didn't tell her when, 4 years after he graduated, he was found strangled with his own belt, and with something like 100 stab wounds, in a motel outside of Dubuque. So there was Dubuque again.

18

Shakespeare.

I think William Shakespeare was the wisest human being I ever heard of. To be perfectly frank, though, that's not saying much. We are impossibly conceited animals, and actually dumb as heck. Ask any teacher. You don't even have to ask a teacher. Ask anybody. Dogs and cats are smarter than we are.

If I say that the Trustees of Tarkington College were dummies, and that the people who got us involved in the Vietnam War were dummies, I hope it is understood that I consider myself the biggest dummy of all. Look at where I am now, and how hard I worked to get here and nowhere else. Bingo!

And if I feel that my father was a horse's fundament and my mother was a horse's fundament, what can I be but another horse's fundament? Ask my kids, both legitimate and illegitimate. They know.

I didn't have a Chinaman's chance with the Trustees, if I may be forgiven a racist cliché—not with the sex stuff Wilder had concealed in the folder. When I defended myself against him, I had no idea how well armed he was—a basic situation in the funniest slapstick comedies.

I argued that it was a teacher's duty to speak frankly to students of college age about all sorts of concerns of humankind, not just the subject of a course as stated in the catalogue. "That's how we gain their trust, and encourage them to speak up as well," I said, "and realize that all subjects do not reside in neat little compartments, but are continuous and inseparable from the one big subject we have been put on Earth to study, which is life itself."

I said that the doubts I might have raised in the students' minds about the virtues of the Free Enterprise System, when telling them what my grandfather believed, could in the long run only strengthen their enthusiasm for that system. It made them think up reasons of their own for why Free Enterprise was the only system worth considering. "People are never stronger," I said, "than when they have thought up their own arguments for believing what they believe. They stand on their own 2 feet that way."

"Did you or did you not say that the United States was a crock of doo-doo?" said Wilder.

I had to think a minute. This wasn't something Kimberley had gotten on tape. "What I may have said," I replied, "is that all nations bigger than Denmark are crocks of doo-doo, but that was a joke, of course."

I now stand behind that statement 100 percent. All nations bigger than Denmark are crocks of doo-doo.

Jason Wilder had heard enough. He asked the Trustees to pass the folder from hand to hand down the table to me. He said, "Before you see what's inside, you should know that this Board promised me that its contents would never be mentioned outside this room. It will remain in your sole possession, provided that you submit your resignation immediately."

"My goodness—" I said, "what could be in here? And what made Tex Johnson run out of the room the way he did?"

"The bottommost document," said Wilder, "was painful for him to read."

"What can it be?" I said. I honestly couldn't imagine how I might have caused Tex pain. When I made love to his wife, I only wanted to make the 2 of us happier. I didn't think of her as somebody's wife. When I make love to a woman, the farthest thing from my mind is whom she may be married to. I can't speak for Zuzu, but I myself had no wish to cause Tex even a little pain. When Zuzu spoke contemptuously of him, I had to remember who he was, and then I stuck up for him.

My first impression of the bottommost document in the folder is that it was a timetable of some sort, maybe for the bus from Scipio to Rochester, a not very subtle hint that I should get out of town as soon as possible. But then I realized that what was doing all the arriving and departing was me, and that the depot, so to speak, was the home of the College President.

The accuracy of the times and dates was attested to by Terrence W. Steel, Jr., whom I had known simply as Terry. I hadn't known his full name, and believed him to be what he was said to be, a new gardener working for Buildings and Grounds. He was in fact the private detective Wilder hired to get the goods on me. What little he had told me about himself may have been invented by GRIOT™, or much of it could have been true. Who knows? Who cares?

He told me, I remember, that his wife had discovered she was a lesbian, and fell in love with a female junior high school dietitian. Then both women disappeared along with his 3 kids. GRIOT™ could have cooked that up.

The timetable about me and Zuzu was signed by the detective and notarized. I knew the Notary. Everybody did. He was Lyle Hooper, the Fire Chief and owner of the Black Cat Café. He, too, would be killed soon after the prison break. That document with his seal was all I needed to see in order to understand that my tenure was down the toilet.

Wilder said that the rest of the papers in the folder were affidavits gathered by his detective. They attested to my having been a shameless adulterer from the moment I and my family hit Scipio. "I expect you to agree with me," he said, "that your behavior in this valley would fall dead center into even the narrowest definition of moral turpitude."

I put the folder flat on the table to indicate that I had no need to look inside. My gesture was like folding a poker hand. In so doing, I would lay it on top of the school's annual Treasurer's Report, one copy of which had been put at every seat before the meeting. I would inadvertently take the report with me when I left, learning later from it something I hadn't known before. The college had sold all its property in the town below, including the ruins of the brewery and the wagon factory and the carpet mills and the land under the Black Cat Café, to the same Japanese corporation which owned the prison.

And then the Treasurer had put the proceeds of the sale, less real estate commissions and lawyers' fees, into preferred stock in Microsecond Arbitrage.

"This is not a happy moment in my life," said Wilder.

"Nor mine," I said.

"Unfortunately for all of us," he said, "the moving finger writes; and, having writ, moves on."

"You said a mouthful," I said.

Now the Chairman of the Board, Robert Moellenkamp, spoke up. He was illiterate, but legendary among Tarkingtonians, and no doubt back home, too, for his phenomenal memory. Like the father of the founder of the college, his ancestor, he could learn by heart anything that was read out loud to him 3 times or so. I knew several convicts at Athena, also illiterate, who could do that, too.

He wanted to quote Shakespeare now. "I want it on the record," he said, "that this has been an extremely painful episode for me as well." And then he delivered this speech from Shakespeare's *Romeo and Juliet,* in which the dying Mercutio, Romeo's gallant and witty best friend, describes the wound he received in a duel:

"No, 'tis not so deep as a well, nor so wide as a church door; but 'tis enough, 'twill serve: ask for me tomorrow, and you shall find me a grave man. I am peppered, I warrant, for this world. A plague on both your houses!"

The two houses, of course, were the Montagues and the Capulets, the feuding families of Romeo and Juliet, whose nitwit hatred would indirectly cause Mercutio's departure for Paradise.

I have lifted this speech from Bartlett's *Familiar Quotations*. If more people would acknowledge that they got their pearls of wisdom from that book instead of the original, it might clear the air.

If there really had been a Mercutio, and if there really were a Paradise, Mercutio might be hanging out with teenage Vietnam draftee casualties now, talking about what it felt like to die for other people's vanity and foolishness.

19

When I heard a few months later, after I had gone to work at Athena, that Robert Moellenkamp had been wiped out and then some by Microsecond Arbitrage, and had had to sell his boats and his horses and his El Greco and all that, I assumed he quit the Board. Tarkington's Trustees were expected to give a lot of money to the college every year. Otherwise why would Lowell Chung's mother, who had to have everything that was said at meetings translated into Chinese, have been tolerated as a member of the Board?

Actually, I don't think Mrs. Chung would have become a member if another Trustee, a Caucasian Tarkington classmate of Moellenkamp's, John W. Fedders, Jr., hadn't grown up in Hong Kong, and so could serve as her interpreter. His father was an importer of ivory and rhinoceros horns, which many Orientals believed to be aphrodisiacs. He also traded, it was suspected, in industrial quantities of opium. Fedders was perhaps the most conceited man I ever saw out of uniform. He thought his fluency in Chinese made him as brilliant as a nuclear physicist, as though 1,000,000,000 other people, including, no doubt, 1,000,000 morons, couldn't speak Chinese.

When I met with the Trustees 2 years ago, and they had become hostages in the stable, I was surprised to see Moellenkamp. He had been allowed to stay on the Board, even though he didn't have a nickel. Mrs. Chung had dropped out by then. Fedders was there. Wilder, as I've said, had since become a Trustee. There were some other new Trustees I didn't know.

All the Trustees survived the ordeal of captivity, with nothing to eat but horse meat roasted over burning furniture in the huge fireplace in the Pavilion, although Fedders would be the worse for an untreated heart attack. While he was going through the worst of it, he spoke Chinese.

I wouldn't be under indictment now if I hadn't paid a compassionate visit to the hostages. They wouldn't have known that I was within 1,000 kilometers of Scipio. But when I appeared to them, seemingly free to come and go as I pleased, and treated with deference by the Black man who was actually guarding me, they jumped to the conclusion that I was the mastermind behind the great escape.

It was a racist conclusion, based on the belief that Black people couldn't mastermind anything. I will say so in court.

In Vietnam, though, I really was the mastermind. Yes, and that still bothers me. During my last year there, when my ammunition was language instead of bullets, I invented justifications for all the killing and dying we were doing which impressed even me! I was a genius of lethal hocus pocus!

You want to know how I used to begin my speeches to fresh troops who hadn't yet been fed into the meat grinder? I squared my shoulders and threw out my chest so they could see all my ribbons, and I roared through a bullhorn, "Men, I want you to listen, and to listen good!"

And they did, they did.

I have been wondering lately how many human beings I actually killed with conventional weaponry. I don't believe it was my conscience which suggested that I do this. It was the list of women I was making, trying to remember all the names and faces and places and dates, which led to the logical question: "Why not list all you've killed?"

So I think I will. It can't be a list of names, since I never knew the name of anybody I killed. It has to be a list of dates and places. If my list of women isn't to include high school or prostitutes, then my list of those whose lives I took shouldn't include possibles and probables, or those killed by artillery or air strikes called in by me, and surely not all those, many of them Americans, who died as an indirect result of all my hocus pocus, all my blah blah blah.

I have long had a sort of ballpark figure in my head. I am quite sure that I killed more people than did my brother-in-law. I hadn't been working as a teacher at Athena very long before it occurred to me that I had almost certainly killed more people than had the mass murderer Alton Darwin or anybody else serving time in there. That didn't trouble me, and still doesn't. I just think it is interesting.

It is like an old movie. Does that mean that something is wrong with me?

My lawyer, a mere stripling, has paid me a call. Since I have no money, the Federal Government is paying him to protect me from injustice. Moreover, I cannot be tortured or otherwise compelled to testify against myself. What a Utopia!

Among my fellow prisoners here, and the 1,000s upon 1,000s of those across the lake, you better believe there's a lot of jubilation about the Bill of Rights.

I told my lawyer about the two lists I am making. How can he help me if I don't tell him everything.

"Why are you making them?" he said.

"To speed things up on Judgment Day," I said.

"I thought you were an Atheist," he said. He was hoping the Prosecuting Attorney wouldn't get wind of that.

"You never know," I said.

"I'm Jewish," he said.

"I know that, and I pity you," I said.

"Why do you pity me?" he said.

I said, "You're trying to get through life with only half a Bible. That's like trying to get from here to San Francisco with a road map that stops at Dubuque, Iowa."

I told him I wanted to be buried with my 2 lists, so that, if there really was going to be a Judgment Day, I could say to the Judge, "Judge, I have found a way to save you some precious time in Eternity. You don't have to look me up in the Book in Which All Things Are Recorded. Here's a list of my worst sins. Send me straight to Hell, and no argument."

He asked to see the 2 lists, so I showed him what I had written down so far. He was delighted, and especially by their messiness. There were all sorts of marginal notes about this or that woman or this or that corpse.

"The messier the better," he said.

"How so?" I said.

And he said, "Any fair-minded jury looking at them will have to believe that you are in a deeply disturbed mental state, and probably have been for quite some time. They will already believe that all you Vietnam veterans are crazy, because that's their reputation."

"But the lists aren't based on hallucinations," I protested. "I'm not getting them from a radio set the CIA or the flying-saucer people put in my skull while I was sleeping. It all really happened."

"All the same," he said serenely. "All the same, all the same."

20

After Robert Moellenkamp, broke-and-didn't-know-it, said so grandly, "A plague on both your houses!" Jason Wilder commented that he did not feel, in the case under discussion, my case, that 2 houses were involved.

"I don't believe there is 2 of anything involved," he said. "I venture to say that even Mr. Hartke now agrees that this Board cannot conceive of any alternative to accepting his resignation. Am I right, Mr. Hartke?"

I got to my feet. "This is the second worst day of my life," I said. "The first was the day we got kicked out of Vietnam. Shakespeare has been quoted twice so far. It so happens that I can quote him, too. I have always been bad at memorizing, but I had an English teacher in high school who insisted that everyone in her class know his most famous lines by heart. I never expected to speak them as being meaningful to me in real life, but now's the time. Here goes:

" 'To be, or not to be: that is the question: Whether 'tis nobler in the mind to suffer the slings and arrows of outrageous fortune, or to take arms against a sea of troubles, and by opposing end them?

" 'To die: to sleep; no more; and by a sleep to say we end the heart-ache and the thousand natural shocks that flesh is heir to, 'tis a consummation devoutly to be wished.

" 'To die, to sleep; to sleep: perchance to dream: ay, there's the rub; for in that sleep of death what dreams may come when we have shuffled off this mortal coil, must give us pause.' "

There was more to that speech, of course, but that was all the teacher, whose name was Mary Pratt, required us to memorize. Why overdo? It was certainly enough for the occasion, raising as it did the specter of having yet another Vietnam veteran on the faculty killing himself on school property.

I fished the key to the bell tower from my pocket and threw it into the middle of the circular table. The table was so big that somebody was going to have to climb up on it to retrieve the key, or maybe find a long stick somewhere.

"Good luck with the bells," I said. I was out of there.

I departed Samoza Hall by the same route Tex Johnson had taken. I sat down on a bench at the edge of the Quadrangle, across from the library, next to the Senior Walk. It was nice to be outside.

Damon Stern, my best friend on the faculty, happened by and asked me what I was doing there.

I said I was sunning myself. I wouldn't tell anybody I had been fired until I found myself sitting at the bar of the Black Cat Café. So Professor Stern felt free to talk cheerful nonsense. He owned a unicycle, and he could